9:41

and other stories

Books by John Nicholas Iannuzzi

FICTION

9:41 and Other Stories
Talion
Condemned
J.T.
Courthouse
Sicilian Defense
Part 35
What's Happening?

NON-FICTION

Handbook of Cross-Examination, the Mosaic Art
Handbook of Trial Strategies
TRIAL: Strategy and Psychology
Cross-Examination: the Mosaic Art

9:41

and other stories

JOHN NICHOLAS IANNUZZI

a MADCAN Book

ISBN: 978-1-5040-4019-8

Distributed in 2016 by Open Road Distribution
180 Maiden Lane
New York, NY 10038
www.openroadmedia.com

CONTENTS

AUTHOR'S NOTE

I graduated from Fordham College, Rose Hill in June 1956.

Following in my Father's footsteps, I entered Fordham Law School in September, that same year. By December 1956 I realized that toiling amongst the dusty volumes of boring law reports was an ordeal of overwhelming proportions; I quit law school. My Father, of course, was sorely disappointed.

For no apparent reason, and with no previous schooling or experience, I began to write—and experiment in writing—setting down, mostly in 1957, the stories recorded in this book. I didn't realize these stories were mental calisthenics, my preparing to steel myself to begin writing novels.

I completed my first novel, *What's Happening?* some time in the fall of 1958. Other than *9:41*, which I wrote the morning my daughter Andrea Marguerite was born in November 1960, I have never written another short story. When I completed *What's Happening?* I had just passed my 23rd birthday.

—jni

9:41

and other stories

9:41

Agony strained through the gritted teeth of the woman lying on the bed. Glenn turned from the window. He gazed down compassionately. Her face was rippled with pain and fear and helpless resignation. Glenn reached for her hand. She loosed her grip on the bedpost and grasped his wrist, squeezing some of her pain into him. He wanted to take more of it, to take it all.

Glenn's eyes slid over her form to the swollen spot in the blanket that was her stomach. Come on. Come on. He thought of the nursery rhyme "Come Out. Come Out", except now is was whatever you are. Come out now. His jaw set hard, angered at his inability to help her, ease her travail.

"It's okay", she murmured, her grip relaxing as pain subsided. Her mouth flickered a vague smile. Her eyes batted closed a couple of times as she began to sink down again into that needed, wanted, half drugged sleep of relief.

Glenn turned to the window again, peering down into the night blackness dotted by streetlights and headlights of passing cars.

Someone knocked softly on the door. Glenn turned. Doctor Moore entered. The Doctor was a tall, slim, middle aged woman with a plain, serene face. She studied the sleeping figure for a moment, then motioned Glenn to accompany her outside.

"Mr. Alexander . . ." The Doctor studied his face. ". . . now she's all right. There's nothing to worry about. It's the normal labor. I don't think, though, that she'll have the baby just yet—not for some hours. She's under heavy sedation, so she'll probably sleep for some time—perhaps two more hours. I don't think she'll have the baby before then. She's doing just fine though". The Doctor's mouth eased into a pleasant, brief smile. Her eyes were soft, understanding. "I'm going to leave for a little while", she said. "One of my brothers passed away. The funeral service is . . .".

"Oh, I'm terribly sorry . . ."

The Doctor smiled more briefly than before. It was a patient, yet tinged with sadness, smile.

"The funeral service is this evening. I'm going to leave for a little while. Your wife is going to be just fine. Don't worry, I'll be back before the baby gets here".

"That's all right. Should I stay here?"

"Well, as I say, she's under pretty heavy sedation. Perhaps you can go and have a little dinner, come back a bit later. When you come back, just knock on the door at the entrance to this section. The nurse will take care of you".

"Thank you, Doctor".

The Doctor turned and walked toward the end of the hall.

A nurse helped Glenn remove the white smock he had been provided and held his jacket for him. He slipped into the jacket and walked through the quiet hall toward the elevator.

A few people sat at the bar, their conversation blending into a monotone of murmur. Glenn sat at the end of the bar, near a window, sitting sideways to look out at the passing traffic. He drank absently, munching on peanuts.

From the corner of his eye, Glenn caught a glimpse of a dark, hunching figure scurrying like a rat flushed from a tenement. The figure darted from the east side of Third Avenue across toward the west side. As Glenn's eyes snared the figure, his stomach tightened.

Something was wrong—something incongruous—traffic was flow-ing—headlights shone all about and bore down on the silhouetted scurrying figure, hunched over, not looking at the traffic. The shadow of the figure and the hurtling juggernaut of cars blended into horrible focus. The figure was going to be run down!! A fantasia of white eyed monsters rose up to surround the frail, running specter. The figure, finally aware, eluded one onrushing car. Good Lord!—another car!! The figure disappeared. There seemed to be a white flash. A woman's pocketbook spun crazily in the air.

"Oh my God—Jesus Christ", Glenn screamed, jumping from his seat.

The bartender spilled a drink on the bar, spinning with fright.

Glenn rushed out the door, looking to where the figure had been, a pocketbook lay in the street. A cab with a crushed hood was stopped in the middle of the street, the radiator fan rapping against some-thing metal, water draining from beneath the engine. Off to the right, another fifty feet in the direction the cab had been going, a twisted, writhing mass lay sprawled on the white line of the avenue. It strug-gled, fought itself to a sitting position. Two men ran to the young woman, helped her to her feet. Each took an arm, supporting the limping, falling, lurching, staggering figure. Her head hung forward inertly on her neck.

"Daddy, . . . oh, Daddy, . . . Daddy", she wailed mournfully. "Help, Daddy . . ."

"Put her down . . . put her down", someone on the sidewalk advised.

"Don't let her walk . . . let her lie there", called another.

A curious crowd milled around, gawking at the spectacle, as the two men eased the figure back down. On closer look, she was only a girl, about fifteen years old, dressed in jeans and a school sweat shirt. A man walking a dog spread his coat over her.

"Ohhh, . . . ohhh . . ." Her pained sobs pierced the murmur of the crowd. The girl's eyes were shut, her head twisting from side to side trying to shake the pain out.

Glenn ran to the light-green metal police call box on a lamp post and jiggled the receiver bar.

"Thirteenth Precinct".

"A woman's just been hit with a car", Glenn shouted. ". . . at Third

Avenue and Seventeenth Street. You better send an ambulance right away. My God—she was mangled. Hurry".

"Your name?"

"What the hell's the difference what my name is—Glenn Alexander—an ambulance. Hurry". Glenn hung up the phone, sure the girl would be dead before the ambulance arrived.

"Ohhh. Daddy. Daddy. Daddy . . .", she screamed in pathetic torment, her head writhing from side to side.

"It's all right, baby. I'm here".

A kid, a boy, maybe fifteen, with sideburns and a square-back haircut, knelt on the street next to her, nervously rubbing her hand. "It's Eddie, baby. I'm here".

The kid was trying to be brave, comforting. He was hardly able to overcome his own fright.

Glenn had seen the boy in the neighborhood before—poor, badly clothed, digging rock and roll, hunched over a little to look tough. This must be her boyfriend, Glenn thought. Poor kid—her insides must be crushed—left only to the frightened sympathy of a helpless kid.

"Call an ambulance. Call an ambulance".

"It's on the way", Glenn called out.

"Ohh. . . ohh . . ." Blood dribbled out of her mouth. Her head rolled from side to side on a newspaper someone placed under her head. Her hair streaked a design in the blood. The right side of her face looked mashed and pulpy, the right eye smaller than the left.

The crowd surged around tight, everyone both grieving and fascinated. Yet no one could relieve or share her anguish one whit. Glenn was rankled by his impotent bystanding at this unshrouding of life.

"Ohh, Daddy, . . . Ohh, help me. please help me . . .".

"Why don't you call her father, Eddie?" Glenn whispered into the boy's ear.

The boy whirled about. "Shh, what's a matter wid you?" He gaped at Glenn. "Her old man died a month ago. Just like that, a heart attack". Eddie's eyes swam with fright.

Glenn's stomach tightened harder with thousands of little, cold knots.

"Ohh. please Daddy, . . . don't let it hurt, Daddy, . . . don't let them hurt me, . . . don't let them hurt me, . . . please don't let it hurt . . . please . . .". She was screaming in agony now.

"It's all right, honey. It's all right, I'm here". Eddie rubbed her hand frenziedly.

The cab driver stood on the side, writing the names of the four girls that had been passengers in his cab. He glanced nervously from time to time at the girl laying on the street. His passengers were young girls, dressed up, going to a Saturday dance or something. They looked a little sick.

"Anybody else see this?" the cabbie asked the crowd. Police sirens cut into the night from far down the avenue. The cabbie rubbed his face nervously.

"I did", said Glenn, walking toward the cabbie. The cabbie scribbled Glenn's name.

Two cops arrived in a squad car. They moved the crowd back, put a blanket over the girl, knelt and inspected her head. The younger cop looked to his partner. He lifted his eyebrows and nodded. The younger cop called the precinct on his car radio, then began asking the crowd for details. The older cop knelt next to the girl, trying to comfort her, watching her wriggle.

Can't anybody do anything for her, Glenn's screamed inside his head.

Finally, an ambulance arrived. The attendants perfunctorily lifted the girl onto the boards of a stretcher.

"Eddie. Eddie, . . . don't leave me. Eddie". She still hadn't opened her eyes.

"Yeah. Eddie's right here . . . here he is", the older cop said absently as he held up one end of the stretcher.

Eddie was looking around, hopelessly, embarrassed, searching for her shoes which the cops had removed.

"Eddie . . . Eddie, my shoes. Somebody took my shoes. Don't leave me, Eddie".

"He isn't leaving", the older cop assured her.

Eddie followed the stretcher to the ambulance, looking on, wondering what he could do.

The red light spun on the top of the ambulance; the siren wailed into the night; the crowd lining the sidewalk hesitated a moment, muttered, and dispersed.

Glenn stood alone; traffic streamed again on Third Avenue. He looked at his watch. The two hours were up. He'd have to get back to the hospital.

It was early morning now. The grey dawn was being forced higher into the sky by the light blue day. Glenn, sitting in the main reception area of the lobby, started to flip through "The Mirror" again for the tenth time, trying to find a story he might have missed. Once in a while, a phone rang softly and a nurse would answer. Occasionally, the vault-like elevator door slid open and soft footsteps disappeared into a corridor.

A cab pulled up to the front entrance. Glenn glanced up and watched as the driver pulled away from the curb and maneuvered back and forth. He stopped several feet from the curb. The cabbie got out and opened the passenger door closest to the curb. An old woman in the cab had crutches. The cabbie lifted her legs one at a time over the door sill and into the street. The woman propped herself up on the crutches, paid the cabbie, then hobbled toward the hospital entrance. Her left foot was twisted away from her body, pointing almost 90 degrees from the direction in which she was headed. Her right leg was thick, bandaged; the bandage seemed soaked with a stain of fresh blood at the shin. She tried to balance herself on the crutches and pull open the door. Wind held it shut. Glenn rushed to the door and opened it.

"Oh, thank you".

She was about 65, a nice wrinkled, grandmother type, with full, smiling teeth. She grimaced as she started the crutches going again. She reached the center of the lobby, looking around. The nurse in her small office off the lobby, could not see the old woman.

"I'll call her for you. You want the nurse?" Glenn asked.

"Would you please". She smiled gratefully. Glenn walked to the admitting office.

"Can you come out here, nurse. A woman's here. She can hardly walk", he whispered.

The nurse, a newspaper spread open on her desk, was annoyed. She was about to tell him to have her come to the office.

"She's bleeding".

The nurse grimaced, relented. She went into the lobby.

The old woman was propped up on her crutches like a straw man on a stick. One of her legs dangled uselessly under her.

"Can I help you, madam?" The nurse scrutinized the bleeding, then peered into the old woman's face for an answer.

"Yes . . . Doctor Chaves. She told me she'd meet me here".

The nurse winced a smile and nodded. "If you'll have a seat. I'll call her".

The old woman grimaced again and swung her left leg forward, moving toward a chair. She stopped with her back to the chair, balanced on the crutches, looking at the chair over her shoulder. She swung her right shoulder back, her weight starting to carry her backwards. Her left arm pivoted her on the crutch and she fell onto the chair. The chair slid back about a foot. The old woman gripped the armrests, then smiled a bit satisfied as the chair stopped sliding. She smiled toward Glenn.

"Thank you", she smiled toward Glenn momentarily. She turned anxiously toward the nurse's room. Fresh blood appeared on her leg. Glenn wondered what horror of a leg was under the bandage. He forced himself to smile back as if he didn't notice her legs.

The nurse's phone rang again. "Admitting office".

A nurse came into the lobby and smiled a little. The old woman looked up anxiously.

"Mister Alexander?"

"Yes?"

She nodded and walked back to the office.

"Yes. Doctor, he's here". She rehung the phone and returned. "Doctor Moore wants you to meet her by the elevator".

Glenn walked toward the elevators. The second hand swung lazily, slowly around the wall clock. It was ten o'clock. The elevator doors slid open. Doctor Moore stepped out. She smiled.

"Your wife had a very difficult time . . . very painful. She suffered a great deal . . . but she's alright". She smiled her smile again. "You have a daughter . . . at 9:41 a.m.".

A strange, cold, empty, hollow feeling flashed through Glenn's body. A tingle slipped up his neck to the back of his ears. He thanked the Doctor and walked back toward the lobby. The woman with the legs was still looking toward the nurse's office anxiously. It begins, for someone new, Glenn thought. He knew he should be happy, jubilant, elated, but somehow there was a gnawing, an ache, for sorrows envisioned, imposed.

CHRIS

The night was aglow with a warmth that makes the world seem to live suddenly and call forth all its elements to awaken; winter is finally defeated. Overhead, in the still sky the stars shone and twinkled with a luminance that was overwhelming and yet frightening. Each little spot of light in the heavens millions and millions of miles away hung silently watching the quiet sleeping world. My footsteps echoed soundly on the hard pavement as I made my way home along the route I took every night, 17th to Irving, Irving to 18th, 18th to 3rd, and 3rd, home. I lived on Third Avenue, always have, I lived there when the "El" cut its way through the teeming, screaming street, and when it was being torn down, and now when it is looked to as the fashion lane to come.

People are strange, and the evolution of a city even stranger. The swank sections give way to newer swank sections, and the lesser rich take over the deserted place, and round and round, never ending until the swank section is the slum of today and is torn down to make way for a new swank section. I like 3rd Avenue, I like it for its rawness, its realities; it is life in all its hardship and degeneracy, and all its sublimity.

As I walked under the street light, the glare made the stars fade from view, and as I passed from under the direct rays of the light the little worlds so far away became visible again. I turned into 19th Street, and found the air filled with the strumming of a guitar. Spanish music filled the air, and the small street was alive with the air of a Spanish Village. The Spanish people, as always, were out on the stoops and sidewalks in front of their buildings, singing and playing their native songs. Across the street, silently sitting, outlined in his window frame was Chris, watching silently, as always, the joys and sorrows of 19th Street. He seemed never to breathe, nor did he stir from his position in front of the window. Chris was as old man, a stern looking old man, who had a countenance that resembled a rock, imperturbable, impervious, ever the same. Chris would sit in front of his window until the very early hours of the morning, just sitting and staring at the people, the music players, and listening to their serenades. Winter would come and give way to the cool breezes of Spring, and thence to the thermal blasts of Summer, thence to the harsh winds that foretell the coming of Fall, but faithful Chris was ever there, grey bearded, and white haired, with a nose that jutted from the middle of his face like an afterthought to a sentence. His skin was white, with a slight hint of color at the cheek bone. It was a very rough skin, wrinkled and aged like fine leather, smoothed through use, and cracking from age. His eyes were steel grey and sparkled like the sun reflected off water. They were the most frightening of all his aspects, and fearsome were they all. They could sear through the most adamant of persons and boil them down to the core of their very being.

I'd known Chris for years; he had been at that window before I was born, so I've heard, and as I grew older Chris was an integral part of my life. Not that I would be with him too often, but he was always near during the early years of my youth, sitting in front of his window to witness the games that we played, the fellows of my youth and myself. He watched us all sprout and grow older and perhaps wiser. He himself was very wise, I knew, for every so often, I, being the most intrepid of my fellows, was friendly with him; a feat which was not unheralded in the gossip of my neighborhood. For Chris was not the most gregarious of human beings, and people feared him as much as they respected him. This friendliness with Chris brought no end of inquiries from all of the people of the neighborhood from time to time. What was he like? Why did he always sit in the window? Who was he? Was he an artist or an exile? Was he insane? Or, as it finally would boil down, just what was this Chris that everyone feared unknowingly.

During my few visits to Chris's home, I was treated most cordially, treatment which at first surprised me emanating from the ogre that lived all by himself and stared out at people that passed by. He lived in a small apartment, inexpensively but neatly furnished. As you entered you saw a couch in the corner, well worn, and covered in a rust colored slip cover that Chris had probably made. The couch was the most prominent feature of the entire room, and upon entering it captured your attention immediately. It lay hung in an almost exotic space, emitting a strange, luxurious aroma, that seemed to permeate the entire room. It was shrouded in shadow, and surrounded by shelves and bookcases filled with books, so dusty as not to have been used in a hundred years. It was the focal point of the room, for nowhere was there a space from which the couch was not completely visible. There were no lights near the couch, and yet it was worn so, that one could almost see the outline of Chris's body lying on it hour after hour. It was a low couch, without arm rests, just a slab, tilted up on one end so that when one was supine on it, his head was raised. Chris would lie on the couch when I went to see him, and I would be granted the special privilege of resting my humble body in that grand exalted place, the place from which so much terror had been hurtled, the chair in front of the window. The sun would stream in the window directly, brightly, and would cut a rectangular spot of white out of the dark, brownish rug, I, sitting with my back to the window would gaze fixedly at this spot of whiteness, with my shadow outlined in the middle of it. Chris would rest in his dark mysterious spot, almost invisible to the sun struck eye gazing at him from across the room. His voice was strong, and vibrant, and deep, and would float and dance around the room until its resonance made the sun spot lift from the floor with me on top of it and soar into the upper reaches of the atmosphere, only to suddenly descend, rest on water, whereupon, I would alight on the shores of some southern isle, with the water cuddling my feet, and the footprints that I left being washed away by the succeeding waves.

Chris was a marvelous story teller, and I would sit entranced for hours on end. His stories were glorious and fascinating, and brave and bold, and teaching. He told me of many things, and of people, and of things far beyond my imagination. He told me of his youth—in the very cold wastes of a foreign country, where it was necessary for him to sleep fully dressed so as not to freeze. When it would be time for me to go, he would get up slowly, and make his way to the door. He would send me off with a "Goodbye sonny, be a good little fellow now, won't you.

Chris was wonderful, and I looked forward with great anticipation to every meeting. As time grew on, his talks became less fanciful and more full of poignance. He would recite from his memory passages of the great authors, Chris loved literature, and would explain the authors meaning, their method. He taught me truth as I had never known before. But soon I left and went away for school. When I would return on semester breaks there would be Chris, faithful guardian, and I would talk to him briefly, but time was so short and had to do so many things. I just never had an opportunity to go in and spend any time with Chris. The closeness that I had had with Chris as a boy was never recaptured, but none the less, I always saw him sitting in his spot, and would greet him. His face would beam as it very rarely did, and an indication of a smile would transmit itself through his full beard. "How are you, sonny", he would say. "Fine Chris, how are you?" "Oh I'm quite well, thank you, what are you doing these days?" he'd ask. And I would tell him "I'm writing". The smile in the beard would deepen. He really loved art and beauty, though much of my work couldn't be called that. He would always ask me to come to his place sometime and read one of my stories for him, and he would say how he knew I would be an author of worth, and how happy he was for me. I would tell him I'd come sometime, but as it happens I have never yet been able to see him. Well one of these days, I'd tell myself, I'll get a moment and then I'll bring one of my stories to Chris.

These thoughts were going through my head as I undressed for the night, and rested from the overtiring world of the outside. As I lay in bed, which was near a window left purposely uncovered so as to see the night above me, I kept thinking of my youth, and of Chris, and the things that he told me, and . . . suddenly a deafening sound had violated the quiet night air and was echoing from the buildings on the street. I bounded from the bed and rubbed a clean spot from the grimy window so I could see out. Below me was a scene of human carnage, a woman lay bleeding in the street, from her middle came blood in spurts, in gushes, in streams, being pumped out of her body with every beat of her heart. Life was slowly being pumped away, and she lay there writhing in a pool of her own blood—policemen came running down the street, and stopped in front of her, trying to make her more comfortable, and less in danger of dying. One of the policemen ran to a call-box on a lamppost near the corner to report to the station house. The other was looking at her, trying to make her more comfortable and, at the same time, was furtively glancing around for some sign of the actor of the act of violence. He was bent over her, now crouching over her, trying to comfort and yet talk to her, his eyes were darting back and forth over the faces of the buildings, now covered with little squares of white on the shadows, and re-shadowed with the forms of people. People swarmed to their windows to see what was the matter, what was down in the street, to see a scene so base and yet so profound taking place.

Ever searching the policeman's eye came to rest on a little black space of window, unlit by a curious square of light, and there in the window was Chris.

Never moving, Chris was still sitting there silently, and yet very aware of what was happening in front of him. The ambulance from Columbus Hospital, which was only down the street, droned its way to the spot on which the woman was dying. The attendants came to help the woman, and as they did, the policeman who had been staring at the little spot where the white beard showed forth from the reflection of the moon, rose and approached the window. Chris, unflinching, sat there to greet him. I opened my window to hear if I could what was going on.

The police were asking him the routine questions as to his name, and if he lived there, and had he seen anything happen outside. He said he hadn't. "Have you been sitting here all the while?", the policeman said. He had, answered Chris. But then you must have seen what was happening, was the woman alone? Was she walking with any one? Chris reiterated that he had seen nothing.

The police were baffled by his insistence of innocence, and became very irate at the unreasonable resistance of this crazy old coot who sat at his window and minded everyone else's business, but didn't know a damn thing when he should. Another squad car came up as the ambulance with the woman inside pulled away. One of the policemen who was questioning Chris went over to talk to the police that were inside the car. After a short talk, the police in the car came out and walked over to Chris, they talked to him and then told him that he would have to come to the station house for more questioning. He agreed to go and to help out as much as he could.

I ran from the window, dressed hurriedly and ran down to help Chris in any way that I could. Being the only friend he had, I felt I should. I arrived just as the door of the apartment building was opening, and Chris was coming out. The people who had gathered at their windows were almost reaching a fury pitch, for this was the first time that any of them had ever seen more than the hairy apparition at the window. He walked out and said he was ready to go, I called to him and my presence seemed to make him more calm, although to others, he outwardly looked as composed as ever. He put his arm out to me and I held him and walked with him toward the police car. The police were walking on either side of us. He was telling me that he had seen nothing. He said he heard nothing but footsteps and a shot, but had seen none of it.

As we approached the police car, his body lurched forward, as the violating sound returned to haunt the silently watching buildings. His body pulled against my arm with a tautness and a jerking that threw me off balance. He became limp in my arms, which I spread to support him. The police began to run for cover, looking for the assassin. I was in the middle of the street trying to support Chris's sagging body, and lower his inert form as slowly as I could to the ground. Chris was dead, never could he tell of the spectacle he had seen, of the murder, or of the murderer, nor could he ever, thought I, poor Chris, poor wonderful, blind, Chris.

CONNIE

A woman walked towards us; not an old woman, but one who looked as if she already had 60,000 miles on her. About her there was an appearance of fading beauty. Her clothes were frilly and garish. You could tell she was high, not much, but just enough to free her from her mortal bonds. As Ed and I approached, she looked at Ed in an obviously coy way, and said,

"Got a light, honey?"

Ed lit her cigarette, and as we continued walking, Ed said: "Hot stuff, eh, pal? Want a little company, probably only cost a couple of drinks".

"It's not quite as funny as all that, Ed," I said. "I happen to know that tramp. I knew her real well, as a matter of fact . . . we were going to be married".

"Are you serious?"

"Yeah . . . that's Connie. She had quite a body then, and a face— wow. Would drive me crazy every time I saw her. Really a fabulous girl".

I was talking to Ed Sawyer, a fellow I had met at the new job I recently began at Franklin Johnson, an importer on Vine Street. Ed and I became quite friendly, sort of buddies at work. We had just started out on a lunch break when we saw Connie. This was the first time I had seen her in about five years, and she sure had changed. The last time I saw her, she was the girl I wanted to marry, and . . . well, it never worked out. Ed and I walked into a drug store and sat down at the lunch counter. Ed began to ask all sorts of questions, and seeing her again like that after all these years, put me in a very melancholic mood. Words began to spew out, seemingly without any effort on my part.

"She and I became friendly about nine months after I came to California", I mused, "that was about seven years ago. She was a tremendously attractive girl then, about five foot two, with a body that was round, soft and fleshy. One that filled out clothes so excitingly. The kind of body that undulated all over when she walked, and made you feel you were going cross-eyed if you watched her from behind. Her face was cute, not beautiful, but real cute. Dark, warm, passionate eyes showed beneath long, thin eyebrows, etched on white, white skin. Her nose was short and straight, and her mouth was small and thin lipped, and felt good when you kissed it. She wore her naturally brown hair long, but tinted a different color to match her moods. She looked good in every color too!

"She was an aspiring actress, you know the bit. This damn town is full of people who are making a name for themselves, or sliding down, or making a comeback, or something. Everybody wants to be a star. Well, Connie wanted to act, to make the big time, she was to be the great new light of the movies. She was so new, the movie makers didn't know her, not yet. We met one day at a little lunch place, something like this. I noticed this fine looking girl sitting at the counter alone. At first I only noticed how zaftig she was, if you know what I mean. Then I noticed the way she was skimping over a burger and Coke, and, well, I don't know how I saw it, but you know how you feel when you think a person doesn't have enough cash to buy a good meal? That's the way I felt. I figured she hadn't eaten since the burger and Coke she had the day before. And, I was right, she told me, after I chivalrously asked her to join me for lunch. I told her I was a stranger to this section of town, and I never liked to eat lunch alone. Since my youth, I told her, I always ate lunch with a maiden aunt, and after her death I left the old ranch in Colorado, came to California, and since haven't been able to enjoy a single luncheon. I didn't want her to feel I was buying her lunch because she looked broke, and I thought my maiden aunt story might cheer her up a bit. She smiled and said she'd love to keep me company".

Ed's nod urged more.

"We talked some during lunch and she told me she was trying to become an actress. She was looking for her first break, and since funds were pretty low, she was glad I had asked her to have lunch with me. I told her I was doubly glad, first because I had done a good deed, and secondly, because in looking more closely at her, she appeared to be prettier than my aunt. We laughed a lot and had a good time, so I asked her to the movies that night. She accepted, and we had a wonderful evening together. I never had a better time with anyone in my life".

"After that we began to see quite a bit of each other. I was working in a public relations place over on Sunset at the time, we would meet after I finished work. She was almost always free. She would spend her day going to a few studios in the morning trying to get some work, or she'd meet someone who might be able to help her, or she'd just see some of her friends, then she'd go to the little rooming house where she was staying and work the switchboard for two hours a day to earn her room rent. That would just about leave her with enough time to make herself beautiful and come to meet me at a little spaghetti joint on Maple Street. We would have dinner, and then go for a walk, or talk, or see a movie. We really had great times those days, and I was glad to have met such a wonderful girl. I was so happy I could hardly concentrate on my work during the day".

"Once in a while, after dinner, she would come over to my place, and I would change, then we'd go out, after which I always took her home. One night, though, she stayed with me at my place. I held her in my arms all night, and when morning came I couldn't bear to let her go. And, well, she never stayed at the boarding house again, not while we were going out together, anyway".

"Go on", said Ed. "What happened?"

"She moved her things to my place, and we became inseparable, almost. We decided we'd get married real soon. This was something new and different for me. I had been with a lot of women before, but

I didn't give a damn about any of them. This time I was flipping out, and I wanted to get married. We were going to get the benefit of a J.P. as soon as it could be arranged".

"As I said, she'd go around trying to land parts and seeing agents that were going to help her. You know from what you read you'd never think there were any nice girls trying to make it in this business. I only mention this so you don't get the wrong impression of Connie. She was a fine woman, a real woman, and she loved me . . . me alone, forever".

"Anyhow, one night she wasn't at the place when I got there, so I just put a couple of records on the turntable, mixed up a batch of drinks, sat down with a magazine, and waited for her. She had gotten a couple of bit parts lately, so I figured she was working a little late this night. After a couple of hours you might be able to figure I was not only a little worried, but a trifle annoyed. I began to imagine all sorts of things, and my nerves started to give. I mixed another batch of drinks and just sat watching the clock and drinking with determination. Finally, about ten-thirty, the key turning in the lock glued me to my seat. She came into the apartment, and as I turned to see her, I thought someone had just put their hand on my head and began pushing downward. I was numbed. She looked at me through bleak eyes. She looked haggard. She looked as I feared she might. Putting herself down in a chair, she began to cry hysterically. 'Oh, baby, baby,' she screamed. I grabbed her by the shoulders and snapped her head back to look at her face. She had been drinking, you could see it, you could smell it. 'Where in hell have you been? What's the matter?', I demanded. She hung in my arms, lifeless, except for the crying. I was starting to crack. What was it, I begged. She gathered up all the energy she had, and looking away, blurted . . .

" 'I went for a drink down at Ciro's with an agent', she said. 'You know, the one I said got me the part in that picture yesterday'.

" 'Yeah, yeah'.

" 'Well, I had one, two, maybe three drinks, and then everything is blank. I don't remember anything except those three drinks, and . . . and . . . oh, baby', she started crying violently.

" 'And what? What?'

" 'I came to and I was in bed with him' ".

Ed was just staring, hanging on every word.

"Ed, somebody grabbed my stomach and twisted, hard. I couldn't say a word. I could no longer breathe. I was dying. I was dead. She screamed and ranted. She was sobbing through gasps about the horrible thing she did to me. 'She didn't want to . . . she didn't remember anything . . . Oh, what she did to me'. I couldn't speak. I think I must have seen blood oozing over my eyeballs. I was going to kill him. I was going to rip him apart, but not now. I couldn't leave Connie, not in the condition she was in. That rotten son-of-a-bitch—the guy, I mean".

"What happened—with the guy?"

"I got to him afterwards, but things between Connie and me were never the same. I went to his office. There he was in front of me, behind his desk. I can see him now, smiling his affable, affected smile, calculated to win you over. You don't know me, I said, but we have a mutual friend. My voice began to leave me. I didn't want to kill him, I didn't want that, not anymore. I had thought long and hard about it and decided killing him wouldn't change things. I just wanted to see the guy. I just had to see the rotten bastard. I couldn't get into a rage again, violence had left me. I had become resigned to what had happened, nothing could erase it. I just wanted to see him. He must have sensed my state of mind, the smile left his face.

" 'Who is that' ", the guy asked.

" 'Connie' ", said I. He shot a nervous glance at me. " 'You know why I'm here? I just wanted to see what a lowlife really looked like. You miserable' . . ."

" 'Now wait a minute, bud' ", he said. " 'Whatever went on, if anything, between any girl and myself is my business, and hers'. His unconcerned yet plaintive way of speaking made my blood boil. For a moment, I couldn't even see. I grabbed blindly and swung my fist with a strength that was not my own. God, I thought I'd kill him with that punch. I walked out, not even pausing to look back. I left him lying there on the floor of his office".

"What about Connie?" asked Ed.

"Well, I was really sick about it, but Connie took it real bad. She didn't draw a sober breath for a week. She just sat looking into space, drinking and crying. I tried to reason her back to reality, "It's okay, baby. It's not your fault". But I couldn't reach her. One day when I got home, she had already left, without leaving a note, a message . . . nothing".

"That's horrible, it really is", said Ed.

"Yeah, and I hadn't seen her since. I heard she was still around, always a little high, never with an enemy in the world anymore, if you know what I mean?"

Ed looked at me blankly, then said: "We better get back to the office". We paid the check and started back.

"You know, Ed", I tried to say as calmly as I could, "I should have killed that bastard agent. He killed two people. You're looking at one . . . you just saw the other.

ONLY A MATTER OF TIME

Flame flickered into life at the end of the match, illuminating the darkened room with a pale, jaundiced glow. Shadows appeared behind objects in front and to the side of me, throwing fantastic, elongated specters on the wall. I inhaled through the cigarette, infusing it with a glowing ember. The match extinguished in the wind created by its flight through the air, and the room again fell into an obscurity of black. I've been sitting on the couch for what seems to be at least an hour. Through the windows I've watched the glow of day die and the cooling shadow of night deepen. It all seems so strange to me now, now that I'm home alone, in the safety and comfort of my apartment, with merely the spasmodic glow of a cigarette for company. Only a few hours ago, we had been together, she and I, and now she was gone, like the silent fleeting of a cat in the dead of night. Many times before, when unpleasantly pressed by circumstances, I have consoled myself with the thought that with a short passage of time all my trouble would be over. That's all life ever pared away to, a passage of time, and no matter how long the passage, each second of consciousness was a second less to wait, . . . one less, . . . another, . . . another.

Be patient, time will pass, it has to. Soon the entire problem will be over, so stop worrying,

I thought to myself. But now my fear of time was mounting. I missed her terribly. I could hardly keep myself in the soft cushiony hold of the couch. I wanted to run to the phone to call her. I wanted to step into the high powered car that sat at the curb awaiting its master and spark it into its mechanical life, that could zoom me to her so quickly. I could stand it no longer. I had to go to her. But no, what would be the purpose of it all. She didn't want to see me anymore . . .

Never to see her, never again to hear her says she loves me, no that was one horrible fate I could not endure. I can't let this happen to me. I'll keep her no matter. I'll never relinquish my hold of her. God. Oh God, please don't let this happen to me. Oh what am I doing, I can't be calling on God to solve all my problems for me, I have to handle this all by myself. But what the hell can I do, . . . now, nothing. I'll just have to sit and wait.

My mind keeps popping off with conflicts. I feel as if I'm going mad. Wait and wait, is that all one has to look forward to in life, sitting and waiting. I still can't believe that all this has happened in so short a time, but then time passes quickly, sometime to our benefit, and sometime not.

We went to the beach this morning, she and I. How strange those words sound together after the entire relationship seems to have evaporated like the smoke from the top of a chimney. She and I had gone to the beach for one of our usual lovely summer Sunday retreats. We would leave early in the morning, usually about nine, when the sun casts its almost blinding cool early morning light, and we'd be sitting on the beach about ten, enthroned in solitary splendor on couches of sand, watching the ocean jester dance his incessant dance for us. We would bring breakfast with us, the stands that dotted the beach would still be closed, still cooling from the sizzling pace of the previous day's business. They, too, stood in solitary splendor, like sentinels guarding the castle of the beach, with the early morning sun dazzling their red roofs and green shutters, throwing long shadows on the sand. We usually would have coffee half and half, she liked it that way, and some cakes or buns. Then we would just lie there feeling the sun in the heavens warming more and more. About eleven-thirty others would start to populate the beach, bringing with them noise and confusion, shattering the regal silence of the beach with shrill chatter and shouts. We didn't mind, though, how could we? It wasn't our beach. That's why we would go early, just to enjoy, even ever so briefly, the magnificence of the silent beach. When it became warm enough we would dash into the sea, swimming and floating endlessly. It was wonderful on those Sundays, both of us enjoyed them so. But now I was never to enjoy another . . .

No, no, this can't be . . . Patience, all will be over in a short time . . . I hope so. I can't stand it much longer . . .

Then we would spend the rest of the day basking in the sun, or playing catch on the sand. Afterward, we would return to our lockers and dress. I would drive the car to the front of the locker section and she would step in, with all her rare, particular beauty radiating. I was proud that she belonged to me. Her singular beauty always turning other men's heads, causing stares and looks of admiration everywhere. I would feel a glow swell up inside every time I saw her coming toward me. She's mine and no one else can every say that, no one, I would always say that. She was beautiful, and today she looked exceptionally wonderful in her gaily printed light blue dress, with abstract design going over the surface of it, with her dark straight hair hanging loosely to her shoulders, held in place only by a slight band of light blue chiffon which encircled her head and ran under the long tresses at the back. She wore the pair of silver earrings I gave her, through the lobes of her delicate ears. All of her features were delicate, all save her eyes. They were magnificent, were grand, they were a pool of luminescence upon which I reflected for hours. They were brown, a warm, sensual, penetrating, understanding, dark brown, which shallowly reflected the sunlight by lightening in color to a tawny shade of velvet. I would gaze at her, entranced, for hours, especially at her eyes, which seemed to enter my very being, probing its hidden inner secrets. These eyes were framed on her soft white skin by arched thin brown eyebrows. Her nose was small and upturned, which gave her the profile of a Grecian goddess. Her mouth was full and ripe, like grapes before harvest. Her chin was small and graceful. She was tall, a quality, which when combined with a liquid, rhythmic gait always seems to give a woman the appearance of magnificent grace. It was wonderful today as we drove home, simply wonderful, as it always was on Sundays . . . but, also, never more shall I be able to enjoy the beauty or the serenity that we shared together . . .

Wait, it's only a matter of time. It won't last forever, . . . I hope

We drove home, and as we usually did, we stopped in the Village for dinner. We stopped at a picturesque little Italian place with red-checkered tablecloths, Italian-looking waiters, and wonderful food. Afterwards, I drove to her house, and then it happened! Everything that had been so wonderful until then, until we got to her place. Then she told me we were never to see each other again. That was the blow I could not withstand. A blow that made me cringe with the fear of reality, cringe and run from the possibility of such a horrible thought. My mind began to grow frantic. I did not expect, nor did I ever suspect that she would find someone else. The thought of this even now makes my mouth grow dry, my stomachache, my jaws grow tense . . .

No, no, it couldn't be true . . . But it is true, that is exactly what she told you. What we had shared for so long was now over, and the enjoyment of it could never be recaptured. She was sorry, but nonetheless, it was true. How could she do this to me, the mean, deceiving, bitch. How could she play me for a fool like that. Does she think I'm an idiot to be made the laughing stock of the world??

I can't recall with all clarity exactly what happened after that, but I must have been so struck dumb by her words, those mean, horrible words, I don't even want to think of, that I couldn't speak. I just couldn't believe what she had told me. I didn't want to. Suddenly I found myself here, where I am now, sitting in the living room, staring at the windows, watching the day die, and the shadows of night deepen. I've been thinking of her, of how I love her, and of how empty life shall be without her from now on. There is no purpose in living for me anymore, for this love is something that time will not pass. I have found, to my regret, that there is something that time will not help to pass, a reality which will always exist, like God, like time itself. It will never pass away but will grow deeper with every passing moment. The cigarette I was smoking was now down to its last few grains of tobacco. I put it out. The door bell is ringing. Who could it be? It is she! She has come back! She has realized that it was all a mistake.

"Just a minute. I'm coming".

As I opened the door my visions of renewed joy change quickly to bewilderment. It is not she; it is two men. What are they doing here? What do they want? Where is she?

"Are you Tiempo Fugita?" they said.

"Yes, I am. Can I help you gentlemen in any way?"

"Perhaps. We're from the police department", they said as they opened little leather folders with badges attached to them. "Did you know a girl named Madeleine Avery?"

"Yes, of course I know her . . . what do you mean did I know her? Is there anything wrong? Did something happen to Maddy?"

"That's what we've come here for. She's dead".

"Dead? No, no, that couldn't be true, not Maddy. What happened?"

"She was strangled to death. Were you with her today?"

"Yes. I left her just a few hours ago. She was alright then".

"You'll have to come with us, Mr. Fugita. We have reason to believe that you killed her. A neighbor heard her scream and then saw you run out of the apartment".

"Maddy dead? I did it? No, no, not Maddy. Not she. Not me. Oh, God, what have I done? I killed Maddy, the only person in the world I cared for? It can't be true. You must be kidding. Please say you're kidding, please".

"I wish we could, mister, but it's true, she's dead. Will you come with us now".

"This can't be true. I couldn't have killed her. No this is all a mistake".

That's all right, keep calm, it can't last forever, whatever the outcome it is only a matter of time and things will be peaceful again . . .

"All right, officers, I'll come, just let me get my clothes".

Relax. Remember everything resolves itself in time . . . patience . . . It's only a matter of time, it can't last forever.

A GLASS OF WINE AND THOU

Soft, warm lazy eddies of air drifted irresolutely past the papers and books as they lay motionless on the desk, motionless save for the infrequent flutter of a paper edge momentarily lifted into life by the wind of the rotating fan, only to be dropped with equal swiftness back to the inertness that marked it before. The windows of the office were open, but their portals were untrespassed by invading air. No wind was stirring. Sun shafted down on the green metal roof of the next building, visibly lifting heat rays from its surface. The sounds in the office were somehow different today, so far away, so muffled, so incapable of intruding as on other days. Perhaps the heat stifled it, as it did the people who were working with an unusual, a low, methodical, almost funereal pace.

I was sitting behind my desk, slouched on the end of my spine, gazing fixedly at the quietness of a little corner, alone, aloof, impregnable, perhaps uninvaded since its construction. Had anyone ever poked into that small corner? How peaceful it must be to exist as a completely independent entity with no care in the world save the support of a wall.

A hard click-click of heels in the outside corridor shook me from my musing. The steps stopped outside and a knock resounded through the wooden door.

"Come in". It was Fran Wilson.

"Hello, Jonathan".

"Any news?" I asked.

"No, not yet. The doctor said it would take a couple of days more".

"Okay, baby. Tell me as soon as you hear, will you? The suspense of it all is unnerving".

"Do you think I'm enjoying this entire thing immensely?" Fran said.

"I know, but it seems to prey on my mind incessantly. I'm a worrier from way back, you know. I can't eat, or drink . . . I get a queasy feeling in my stomach every time I even taste a morsel of food. I must have lost ten pounds in the last week, and God knows, I can't afford to do that".

"Baby, I don't want you to worry or lose weight, you'll spoil that pretty body and fact. You know, you're a handsome bastard".

"Come on, you can cut that out now, can't you?"

"Well, anyway, I know I'm pregnant, believe me. But you don't have to worry. I want the baby".

"No, no, you don't want the baby. You can't want it. Are you crazy?"

"Yes, about you", she replied, "and I want your baby. At least that will be mine, and no one will steal it away. I'll be able to hug it, and kiss it, and look into his beautiful big brown eyes and think of you. He's going to be a beautiful baby".

"I can't help being mad about you. You make me feel like the greatest guy in the world when you talk, and yet I feel like the world's biggest heel for messing things up like this for you".

"You didn't mess anything up. I wanted the baby, and now I'm going to have it. Jean may take you away from me, but no one will take my baby".

Beads of perspiration swelled up and felt like fuzzy thorns on my temples. I couldn't talk to this girl sensibly. Sure she wanted the baby, but she didn't know what she was talking about. How the hell could she want to have a baby so much, she was only 24, unmarried and unhappy except, she says, when she's with me. I'm sorry I ever let her have a drink with me that night. Want's a baby! She must be mad".

"Who's going to support him?" I asked. "I certainly can't. Oh, not that I can't, but why, who needs this. I can't see any sense to it, especially when it's so easy to take care of".

"You have nothing to do with this baby. It's mine. And you don't have to worry one damn bit about it, you and your Jean. Go on, go on, go running to Jean. I'll take the baby".

"Look, you're going to make life as miserable for another person just as it was for you. Do you really feel that's fair? He'll hate me every waking morning. And suppose you want to get married. Then what?"

"I'll marry somebody who'll love my baby as much as I will".

"No, no, it just won't work. I can't let you do it".

"You can't very well stop me either, can you?"

"No, I guess not. But, oh hell, it's like talking to a brick wall".

"That's right, so why don't you just forget it and let's go to your apartment for a drink. A nice refreshing drink", she said, a guileful smile playing on her lips.

Taking my coat off the hook, I watched her walk to the little sink in the corner of my office. In the mirror above it, she began to smooth her eye shadow and comb her long black hair. As she was fixing her make-up, I, leaning against the wall with my suit jacket folded over my crossed arms, slowly and methodically viewed her. She was certainly beautiful, with long hair, and a body bordering on the maddening. Long graceful lines that swelled inside the tight clothes she wore. A derrier that pouted out just so nice, and breasts that glared at you audaciously. Her face was smooth and soft, with warm eyes that shone with love and vixen at the same time. Her mouth was full, like two most strands of rolled dough colored red. That's the word for them, doughy, soft and doughy. Her nose was short and straight and firm and sat there and complemented her face like a nose should. Fabulous. A girl who could get anything, anything out of life, and here we are, she so beautiful, primping in front of a mirror in my office, and me, feeling like a rotten bastard because I feel I've thrown more salt on the wound life has already inflicted upon her. And yet, I feel she should feel sorry for me. She, whose parents didn't want her, she, who lived in foster homes with strange people to care for her, or not, as they pleased. She, who lived in a prison-like orphanage for two years, she, whose life was filled with violence and harshness and unfeelingness, who never really loved, and had never really been loved, who needs life to live, life of and for, she should pity me who feels incapable at her feet, incapable of being as strong or as sure of my life as she. I, who cannot understand her wanting the baby, inside knowing the reason why. At last she will have something to love and call her own, to love and to know the returned feeling is warm and sincere as it has never been in the past. She wants someone to replace me, now that she knows we can never be closer, never share life as she wanted to. Why the hell did I ever happen into her life to mess things up for her; why the hell did she fall in love with me? I could never give her that which she should have.

Fran turned from the mirror, took my hand in hers, and we started for the door. The elevator door opened and we stepped into a mechanical agent of another world. The doors closed on the world of business; I no longer existed there save for my name on the door of the office. We descended down the shaftway to the other world, the world of concrete and steel, of people, and noise, and small. The doors opened and we strolled out toward the sidewalk. I signaled for a cab that was down the street. The driver saw me and his machine veered to my direction. Suddenly an interloper leaped between two cars and hailed the cab. The cab slowed, the interloper got in and rode away. I turned with a shrug to Fran who was standing on the sidewalk. She was looking at me with that soft look in her eyes.

"Let's walk a couple of blocks to The Outpost and get a drink, okay?" I asked.

"Sure, let's go", she said.

We walked slowly, she leaning on and holding my arm at the same time. "What are you doing tonight?" she asked.

"You know damn well what I'm doing tonight, why ask? Why do you make me say things that hurt you when you already know the answer?"

"I don't know. Maybe it will hit me some day that you're married and I'm wasting my time". She turned to the front and kept looking straight ahead, a most look predominating her features.

"Now don't start crying, please. I've told you there's nothing in the world worthy of your tears, especially me".

The Outpost was a cool, lush little place with dim lights, cold powerful drinks, and noisy people. The smart set in their uniforms of three-button, unadorned, Brooks specials, with Madison Avenue crash helmets smacked on their heads irrespective of their shape or size.

"Come on, let's wade through the boys and find us a seat", I said.

We sat at a corner booth and I gave an order. I just sat there in the cool air, still moist under my jacket from the weather outside, thinking of the first time Fran and I sat here, eight months ago. I don't know how it happened. She was just a girl at the office. We had a drink together. I knew she liked me, but I couldn't help that. That was the beginning, and it hasn't ended yet. Another drink, perhaps a movie, a lift home, another drink, a late night at the office to Jean, the beginning of an affair to Fran. It just persisted, so nice, so warm, and yet, underneath it all, so meaningless. I couldn't really love Fran; it was . . . perhaps she pleased my ego, made me feel good when she raved about me the way she was prone to do. I don't know. All I do know now is how rotten I feel about the entire affair. And Jean, how badly I feel when I think of her. I think the best action on my part would be to shrink out of sight and sort of silently drift from the entire picture.

Cold drinks, cooling, and yet, inside, they made me morose and warm, dulled my objectivity, made me a sentimentalist.

"Let's go, baby", I said as I paid the check. We went outside and I hailed a cab. I gave the driver the address and leaned back against the stiffly covered spongy seat.

Fran leaned against me, not saying a word. The cab eased to a stop in front of the address I had given. We got out and went inside. My little apartment, just mine. Jean didn't even know I had it. I paid a minimum of rent and had a nice place to have a drink, or rest . . . or a baby. We went inside and I got a bottle of wine out of the cooler while Fran changed into the axiomatic 'more comfortable'.

I went into the bedroom and was changing into some slacks. Fran came in with the bottle of wine and two glasses.

"What are you doing, going to leave already?" she queried.

"No".

"Well, what are you dressing for?"

"Oh baby, you're out of your God damn head".

"What he hell, it can't make things worse", she said.

"Look, I don't think you're pregnant, so why take another chance?"

"I am so, so forget about it. Let's have some wine".

I took the glass she handed me and sat down on the side of the bed.

Flickeringly, I opened my eyes and caught view of the empty wine bottle lying carelessly thrown on the floor. The room was dimmed with only the light from the fading day to illumine our illicit interlude. I twisted onto my back and as I did I felt the smooth warmness of Fran's leg on mine. I propped myself up on one elbow and with my free hand smoothed a loose strand of her hair that had fallen over her forehead. She restlessly stirred and her eyes opened. She batted them closed and open a couple of seconds and then kept them open, looking at me. She smiled.

"Hello, lover", she said.

"Hi".

I was feeling relaxed and happy. I was lying there completely at ease, thoughts of Fran and her love making on my mind. Suddenly the thought of the baby, or at least of Fran's overdueness splintered my mind like a dum-dum bullet. My happiness disappeared and I was left with only remorse; remorse not only for the possibility of a baby, but also for the thoughts I had about wanting to destroy it, and now, more pointedly, about continuing to lie with Fran and causing something to exist if it did not already. I couldn't resist her. I was drawn every so quickly into the swirling water of a whirlpool that surrounded her, and I resisted not. Fran slid her arm over my chest and held herself against me.

"I think I'd better get going, baby".

She tensed throughout. An electric shock seemed to pass through the arm that lay on my chest.

"Oh, now you're going home to your dear wife, you son-of-a-bitch. Can't you just break with her? Why don't you leave her? You don't even buy me dinner, you bastard".

"Stop the nonsense. You know the damn story backwards, and yet you come back for more, so why bitch about it?"

"Why shouldn't I bitch?"

My mind was weary from this age-old argument. Every time I left for home I heard it. And now with thoughts of Fran being pregnant, I was not very receptive to argument. I swung my legs over the side of the bed, grabbed my clothes from the chair and stormed into the bathroom. The sprawling wine bottle slid under my feet and my legs twisted beneath me. I stumbled across the room to the accompaniment of "good for you, you bastard".

I got into the shower and let the cold water run over my head.

I was standing in front of the lowered blind in the window of my office. Horizontal slats cut across my field of vision. The slats were shadowed and out of focus, while through them I could see people streaming back and forth over the pavement, bustling and hustling. Fran slipped her arm through mine.

"Hi", I said, surprised. "I didn't even hear you come in".

"I know". She rubbed her head against my shoulder. "Look what I have". She was redolent with a perfume she always wore. I took a pink slip of paper from her and began to open it. On top, it read. Dr. Jason Drager, with an address and other business information. I realized this was the report. My fingers nervously began to fumble with the folded edges of the paper. There was one word on it . . . "positive". My stomach that had been queasy for a week, now felt as if it were three yards deep. I felt a completely empty, cavernous, lonely, sick feeling there. My head grew a little weak and began to throb. Fran smilingly told me that she told me so.

"Oh no, no, oh, I've got to do something about this. Look, baby, let's go to some doc who will fix things up for a fancy price, okay?"

"Nothing doing. You're not going to take my baby away from me".

"But be reasonable. How will you be able to support him. How will you be able to go out to work, or even on a date? You have so much of life yet in front of you and to want to throw it away and play nurse for the rest of you life. There's still time enough to do something about it. Later may be too late".

"You just don't worry about it. I'll go away and I won't even give him your name. I won't even tell him you're his father".

"But how unfair are you being to the child? No father. No one to care for him except you". This was a frightening thought. Fran was a girl who might be interested in something for a while and then would forget about it completely. I could just imagine the child with her. "It wouldn't be fair, and after you have this child, perhaps you'll no longer be in love with me, and then you won't want it. What will you do, put it in a home, like your mother did to you? That's a vicious cycle. A violation of nature that grows deeper and more insidious with every passing generation".

"I'll take care of it. What are you worried about. You won't have to pay for it".

"I'm thinking about the child right now". This argument will persist interminably, I'm sure of that. Poor little kid if she ever get's him.

It's been almost a week and I haven't heard any further word. I haven't been able to reach Fran on the phone. 'Where in hell did she go now?' I thought. All I do is sit and call, and wait, and worry, and frantically search for an answer to this situation. There doesn't seem to be one. I couldn't really bring myself to suggest her taking some kind of pill or have an abortion. It just wouldn't be right. It's murder, plain and simple. I couldn't conscientiously do it. But what then? Let Fran have the baby? Poor little kid. The phone rang. It was Fran. Her voice sounded strained yet welcome as it filtered through the ear piece. She asked me to go over to her place.

"What for?"

"I just want you to come over. Can you?"

"Yes. I'll be over".

I arrived at her place and found the front door unlocked, as usual. She was in the bathroom, busily applying cosmetics. The door was ajar, and there she stood in her bra and panties in front of the mirror, humming. I tapped on the door lightly and she wheeled and smiled.

"Hello, baby", I said.

"Hi. All set to take me out for a drink? Or shall we go over to your place for some wine".

"I hadn't planned on it; out is okay. Where have you been for the last few days? What did you want me to come here for?" I had the feeling that something was in the air, something had happened to make her call.

"I had my period, that's where I was. I couldn't face it".

My entire body was unreasonably unshaken by the news that I had been wanting to hear for days. I just stood there looking at her as I had done on many an occasion, and matter-of-factly said: "That's good". That's all I could say. I didn't feel elated, or happy, although I should. I just stood there and said, "that's good". She turned back to the mirror and gave herself one final look and then came out to slip her dress on. Slowly, I felt a warm sensation wriggling up my back I was beginning to get the impact of the situation. The warmth crawled over the back of my neck. No baby. No baby. The problem is over. I won't have to be a murderer, or the father of a bastard. No more worries, no more cares. A song drifted through my mind. I don't have to kill anyone, or be guilty the rest of my life. Thanks, Lord. I don't know if you helped on this, but thanks. I'm free, free. I felt very light on my feet. I dancingly reached for the phonograph and spun a record. The music lifted high and loud, but I was too elated to really listen. It just formed the backdrop for the dance my mind was dancing . . . it's wonderful, marvelous . . .

"Baby, let's go for a drink". She came out of her bedroom all dressed and ready. We started for the door and were off.

The Outpost was inhabited as usual by a good crowd of people. We found a little table and I ordered doubles. I felt like ordering doubles for everyone in the place.

Fran slipped her arm though mind and leaned on my shoulder. She looked sad. "Happy now, aren't you?"

"Yes, actually, I am".

We had two drinks each. The air in the place was chill, the smoke and the drink warm, my mind happy. Fran, though sad, looked at me as lovingly as ever. I felt like a giddy school boy that has been let out for summer vacation.

"Let's get out of here, baby", I said. The drinks were going to my head. I felt that warm sensation I felt on my neck before all over my body, but now the alcohol added to it. We hailed a cab and got in.

"Let's go out and celebrate tonight, okay?" I said.

"I'm not celebrating, but I'd love to go out with you".

"Great. I'll drop you off and you can change. I'll be over in an hour".

"You don't have to. I'm dressed well enough to go out. Or don't you think so?"

"Sure, you look great". I directed the driver to my apartment. "You know how wonderful I feel, Fran", I said as we alighted from the elevator.

"Yes, I know", she said flatly.

"Let's have one of those nights we used to. Let's enjoy ourselves like we did when we first met. I'll reserve at table at Rao's and we'll go there and eat".

She just looked at me and squeezed my hand a little harder. "Yes, oh yes, that will be wonderful".

We went in and I went to my room and began to change. I was filled with a warm and effervescent glow. "La, la, la, la, la . . ." Fran came into the room with a cool bottle of wine and two glasses. She was looking at me with her warm passionate eyes as she handed me a glass of wine. The whirling music stopped. I just gazed at her eyes as if in a trance as I backed toward the bed and slowly sat down.

THE SCEPTER OF THE SUN

The sun filtered through the trees with a golden brightness as Reggie Moore made his way to work, as he did each morning, across Kensington Square, down Arrow Street, to a little white-washed brick building that served him as an office. Laboratory would be quite the more proper word for it since Reggie was a scientist. Not as you would ordinarily think of a scientist, with glass vials and such, but more on the science-fiction type character one would read about in a magazine. Reggie was perfecting a time machine. Not an out-of-the-world type, fantastic machine, but an honest to goodness time machine, which could, by stepping up the rotary powers of the negative molecules in the atoms of an object, send it to another time in space where the world would exist as it did yesterday, or as it will tomorrow. Many of his fellow scientists thought that Reggie's idea was impractical and even impossible, but, undaunted none-the-less Reggie approached a bright tomorrow, or yesterday as the case may be. He fumbled for his key and upon finding it, opened the door and went in to begin a day's work on the almost completed machine. "La, la, de, dum, dum. Good Morning, Margaret. Did anything come in this morning's post?"

"Yes, Sir, one letter from the English Scientists Association, an invitation to the annual dance".

"Oh, bosh, they're such terribly drab affairs, but then one must keep up appearances, mustn't one?"

"Yes, Sir".

"I'm going down to the basement to work the finishing touches of the machine, and then, ah, and then, my dear, we will be able to project objects backwards and forwards in time at our pleasure".

"I hope you will find everything in order, Sir. I've laid out all the tools I thought you would want".

"Thank you. I'm sure everything will be satisfactory. Please do not disturb me at all for the rest of the morning".

"Very good, Sir".

As he walked down the stairs, Reggie began mumbling. "I do hope I won't hit any snags this morning. I'm sure if I don't I shall be completely finished within two hours. How absolutely smashing, in two hours I'll be finished with almost three year's research and work." He reached the door marked "private", unlocked it and went in. On the table, as the fluorescent bulb blinked on, could be seen a cylindrically shaped metal contraption about three feet high, and about a foot in diameter, with wires protruding from the top, five large dials set on the side near the top, and a small door just below the dials. This was a small-size time machine, a mere toy compared to the ones Reggie planned to build as soon as he perfected this one. Reggie donned his work clothes humming to himself. He lovingly touched the machine, set it on its side, opened the door and began to fumble with the wiring on the inside. At about twelve-thirty, after two and a half hours of most intense work, Reggie announced to himself that the work was finally complete. He pressed the button on the intercom, a buzz came to life, and Margaret's voice said: "Yes, sir?"

"Margaret, come down quickly, I'm all finished and am about to begin the first experiment".

"Right away, Sir".

He beamed with pride at the shiny cylinder in front of him. Then he took one of the white mice he kept in the cellar out of it's cage and was placing it in the machine as Margaret came in. "Here we are, Margaret, on the threshold of a new era in science".

"Quite, Sir".

"I'm going to set the machine for the 17th century. I'm sure they had mice in those days too, wouldn't you say?" he said lightly.

"Yes, Sir".

"I say, Margaret, you don't seem to be the least bit enthused about the entire thing. What is the matter?"

"Well, Sir, it's like this. I've been working for you for two and a half years now, Sir. Every day you come in and work on the machine, and with all the other scientists saying you're balmy, . . . well by this time, Sir, I'm somewhat wondering if this machine of yours really will work".

"Margaret, I'm surprised", he said, looking at her crossly, actually hurt. "But nonetheless, your fears will completely disappear in about two minutes. Watch!"

He closed the door of the machine on the frightened mouse, set the dials at the exact time that he wished to send the mouse to, and threw the power switch. Whirr, the machine's parts began to mesh and pick up speed. The noise began to be a whine, and then a small bell sounded.

"There. Now we shall see, Margaret". He opened the door in anticipation and curiosity. Margaret leaned in a little closer so as to see inside the machine. Reggie peered into the machine. A wry smile rippled across his face as he turned to Margaret. "You'll notice my dear there is nothing inside the machine, nothing at all, whereas only a few moments ago there was a live mouse".

"It really does work. Can you ever forgive me for doubting you for even a minute, Sir?"

"Certainly, Margaret. I'll admit the machine did sound a little fantastic, but I was quite sure that it would work. After all, nature is very consistent, and when the proper steps are taken, success is guaranteed. I really think this is wonderful. I'm going to try it again".

"Oh, please do, Sir. It really amazes me to see such a wonder in operation".

Reggie placed another mouse in the machine, closed the door, and turned the dials. "Now, power on, and . . ." The machine didn't start. "What in hell, don't tell me something has gone wrong already. He reset the power switch at zero and opened the machine. The furry little white mouse inside scampered around the bottom of the machine. Reggie snared it and placed it back inside the cage. "Hand me the flashlight, will you, Margaret?"

"Yes, Sir. What do you think could be wrong with it, Sir?"

"I don't exactly know, probably a loose wire inside or something". Reggie was peering inside the machine, probing from spot to spot with the light beam of the flashlight. "Aha, here we are, just as I suspected, a loose wire. Hand me the small screwdriver please, Margaret".

She handed him the tool; he began to tighten the wire, one hand turning the screwdriver, the other holding the light.

"Oh damn, I can't get at it this way". He placed the light down on the inside of the machine, focusing it on the spot where the loose wire hung and with both hands began to tighten the wiring. "One more turn and . . . there we are. I think that should take care of it". He straightened up, closed the lid, set the dials and threw the power switch. The small engine purred and spun into life. "There we go, now let's get that mouse and see if the machine still works".

Margaret was hurriedly fetching the mouse from it's cage when Reggie looked to her in a befuddled way and said: "Margaret, did you see what I did with my flashlight?"

The bright, orange light of the evening sun as it sat low on the horizon filtered in streams through the gaps in the immense cloud of dust that was raised by the passage of thousands of pairs of sandaled feet sauntering home from the Circus of Nero at the conclusion of the day's games. As the crowds wended their way toward the outskirts of Rome, a slight figure was fighting through the crowd back toward the city. It was a woman, dressed in the unpretentious garb of a plebian, crying with all her might, "Domitius, Domitius, where are you?" She was calling to her son who at the moment was where she was not. Frantically, she ran and walked and ran again when the breath allowed her to, constantly calling "Domitius". About a half-mile further back on the Via Appia, an attractive small boy of thirteen sat on a small grey-veined rock at the side of the road, absorbedly scrutinizing an object he had picked up.

His black hair hung n points over his bronzed face, his dark eyes darting over the shiny object in his hand. It was an interesting, yea, even more, most marvelous thing that he had found. Surely there was not another tube like this in all of Rome, for he, being a vendor of wine skins, having traveled the length and breadth of the entire city, including the outskirts, had never seen another. Never had he seen anything in all of Rome that was so different, so shiny, so strange.

It was a small, tubular object, approximately 7 inches long and 2 inches in diameter, with a black metal body, and a silver tip at both the bottom and top, and a knob like bump on its side, a thin metal circle on one end, and beyond all wonders, a transparent hard shiny substance on the other end with a small eye surrounded by silver inside of it.

"By Jupiter, this is a wondrous thing, though yet, I know not what it is for. I'm sure it is mysterious and wonderful. Perhaps a lost gift of tribute for Nero, or perhaps the lost booty of a Praetor. I think it best I make no mention of this to anyone, even my Father and Mother".

As he concealed his new found curiosity beneath his garments, he heard from afar his name being called aloud. For the first time in many minutes, he realized that the crowds were gone, as was his Mother. He recognized his mother's voice and began to run toward it, calling in return, "I'm coming, I'm coming".

He reached his Mother who was weeping from worry and exhaustion as she stood in the middle of the road.

"I'm sorry I caused you worry, Mother. I just stopped to tie my sandal and I saw many curious rock formations and merely stayed to examine them".

"I was frightened that you might have been run over by those wildly charging horses and chariot. Those rich young madmen from the city care not for the lives of a few poor people as they enjoy themselves while killing us".

"I'm all right, Mother. Let us start for home lest it get dark before we get there".

As they walked along with swift pace, Domitius was driven not by a fear of the dark, but by a desire which deepened with ever stride he took, for underneath his outer garment there beat against his side with every step toward home, the hardness and coldness of that strange metal tube he had picked up at the side of the road. His curiosity began to slip ordinary bounds as his mind was frantically thinking of things that this metal tube might be.

Just as the dark grey of falling night was giving way to ebon darkness, they reached their small, hut-like home, where Casua, the lord and master of their little swelling, sat surrounded by leather goods and sewing equipment, making wine skins for Domitius to sell in the city.

Casua was crippled, hacked down by a sword in the Gallic wars so many years before. He was unable to walk, and had to be carried from place to place. As they entered, he addressed his small family in an annoyed voice.

"Did Nero gorge himself on the sufferings of those poor Christians? I wish to Jupiter he would stop this barbaric pastime. I care not for Christians, but ye gods, I've seen enough suffering, as has all Rome, to enjoy this spectacle. I wish I had the power to stop it".

The family sat down without further talk, and began to eat of the meal Meverina, wife of Casua and mother of Domitius, had just prepared. It was a simple repast of fowl and herbs, with a thick sweet sauce that Casua liked so much for the after-meal sweet.

Domitius ate little during the meal, and that which he did eat, he ate quickly, for he wished to spend as little time as possible in the house. He wanted to get out to the small clump of trees that had been the place of boyhood fantasies, where he knew he would be alone, and there examine the tube with more care.

Once out of the house, he ran, lantern in one hand, the other holding tight the spot where the tube was, so it would not bang against his body too hard, to the hidden place. There, he flung himself upon the ground, and with gasping breath, removed the tube from its hiding place.

"Wonder of wonders, this is a most marvelous thing, whatever it is. It must be a scepter of the gods". He held it sideways, upside-down, twisted it around, felt poked, and prodded every inch of the metal surface. He twisted the end with the metal circle and found that it untwisted from the rest of the tube. This he did cautiously, only to find two smaller tubes within. These were covered with a parchment-like substance and had figures painted in a foreign language. Perhaps a message from the gods.

"Great Caesar, this is a strange thing".

Quickly, he replaced the two smaller tubes to their original place, not wishing to disturb anything should he be found with this treasure. He kept fingering the tube. Suddenly his finger which was on the knob on the side of the tube slipped forward and. . . "Great gods!"

He dropped the tube in astonishment, bolted and ran as fast as he could toward the protection of a big rock. There he sat with a cold moisture spreading over his body, his teeth chattering, his hands shaking.

"Great Jupiter protect me from this horror". He sat where he was in the coldness of his fright for what seemed to be many minutes, not daring to stir. With no further sound, or sign from where he had dropped the tube, he timorously lifted his head above the rock to see what was there.

"Gods on high, protect me". There in front of him, lying on the ground, was the tube he had just been holding in his hands, and emitting from the front of it, from the little eye, was a beam of light . . . a light brighter than the sun, which illumined a path across the little knoll and rested upon a tree in a found circular patch of light.

He stood, petrified behind the rock, silently observing the phenomenon that was taking place in front of him. Certainly this, thought he to himself, was an omen or a sign from the gods. Perhaps it was meant for me to find.

He slowly moved from his hiding place to a spot directly behind the tube, opposite the tree that was being lit up by this marvelous omen from Apollo, the sun god. He crept quietly ever forward until he stood over the tube. It moved not. Now he reached down with trembling hand and picked it up. Still it moved not. He held it in his hand, and as his hand moved, so did the patch of light, now over the ground, now over the trees, making everything before him visible to the eye even though it was darkest night. His trembling fingers pushed the knob on the side again, and suddenly the darkness of the night surrounded him. A great fear overcame him as he stood there with the quietness of the night enveloping him. His curious fingers pushed forward on the knob and again a flash of light jutted out from the little eye and lit up a green fir tree. He pushed the button again; the light went out; again, the light went on; again, the light went out.

"I can control this magnificence with the touch of a finger. What a wonderful gift. Surely the gods sent this to me so that I might control it and use it for some purpose", he thought. "Perhaps enough power to overcome the atrocities that Father was speaking of before. Surely this must be the answer. Power from the gods to withstand the divinity of Nero. It is an omen for me to oppose Nero. Was he not only a few years older than I am when he ascended the throne? So be it, oh gods, I will follow your wishes".

In the days and weeks that ensued, Domitius revealed his power only to a few people, and these that he did show it to were the leaders of the tribes and groups that clustered together for protection. Each of these leaders were astounded by his magnificent gift, and were moved to agree with him as to its purpose. Slowly, a movement began to form. People would gather and Domitius would come with his 'Scepter of the Sun' and shine it forth on the people so that they might receive strength from the sun.

All of these meetings were held at night, in the woods, for "The Light", being of the sun, was not stronger than the sun, and, therefore, could not shine brighter in the day-light than the light that illumined the world, and as there was no place big enough to hold all of the people indoors, the meetings were out in the open at night.

Soon, the movement numbered 10,000 people, including Christians, Jews, plebeians, all of the poor and oppressed. Rumors began to stir on the Palatine Hill that there was a revolution brewing, but Nero was somewhat unmoved to the danger that it presented. Nevertheless, he perfunctorily sent the royal guard out to uncover and disperse this rabble. Domitius and his followers however, were quite careful and clever about their meetings and the guards could never discover their whereabouts.

The Envoy of the Sun, as Domitius was now referred to, and his power of light was becoming a password in the city. Nero was becoming more frightened each day as fresh rumors would start to circulate. The rumors told that this movement was to lay waste the Imperial palace and rid the Roman world of the evil that came from there, including Nero.

Shortly thereafter, Nero began to grow impatient with the royal guard and called upon his army to find and destroy this insidious and treacherous impersonator of divinity. One evening when the royal festivities were about to begin, a runner, one of the army's messengers, came pantingly exhausted to Nero's quarters and told of the movement that had entered the city from the western gate. It was a vast crowd, growing larger with every meter it moved, carrying torches, and at its head was a boy. A mere youth with all the innocent appearance of the young, but in his hand he carried a light, a small light, the path of which he could direct at his wish. A light brighter than the sun.

"Did not the army kill this boy and disperse the crowd?" asked Nero.

"They tried to, Divinity, but when they did, he, the boy that is, threatened to shine the light on them and strike them dead. They all fell back with great fear in them".

"Where is this sun god now, runner?"

"He and his followers are headed here, Divinity".

"Here?" Nero twirled and bolted for the balcony. From this vantage point he could see out across the shadowed roofs of the city. Not more than half a mile from the palace, marked off by the flaming torches they carried in their hands, the crowd could be seen. A faint roar could be heard from them as they proceeded toward the palace. Reports kept coming to Nero . . . "they're approaching" . . . "they're increasing in number". . . "they're laying waste the entire city as they come forward". The crowd was venting all its rage on innocent Rome, the city. The western quarter of the city was already starting to burn.

Nero looked to the west and there, against the back-drop of purple he saw the orange glow of the conflagration. The crowd was only a few blocks from the palace now.

"Guards, the army, send someone out there to stop them, do you hear me!" shouted Nero.

Men of the army issued forth from the front of the palace and stationed themselves in phalanxes across the front entrance. The roar of the crowd was deafening, drowning out all other sounds, including the orders shouted by Nero. The yellow-orange glow of the burning torches could be seen slowly creeping over the ground ever nearer the palace. From the high balcony, Nero saw the shadows of the first part of the crowd as they entered the square. All that could be seen was a yellowish glow and weird out-of-shape shadows of men. Then, around the corner of the wall, came the darkened figures of the first members of the crowd silhouetted in orange. The entire mass of the main body came surging around the corner like a huge, black cloud of dust.

The yelling and screaming was terrifying, yet Nero heard it hardly at all, for in the midst of this entire ebon mass were two spots of light approaching with and just a little ahead of the crowd. One was on the ground, large and oval shaped. The other was suspended in the air a few feet behind. These spots swayed and moved as if they were part of the walking crowd. Nero realized that this was the Scepter of the Sun, Domitius, the sun god. He froze in his position at the edge of the balcony, hands leaning on the parapet, body hunched forward to view the crowd below him.

The light stopped swaying. It emitted from the tube and lit a circle of the red brick in the courtyard. Then, the light which had been traveling in a circular path on the ground in front of the crowd, ventured forward, across the ground further away from the crowd, toward the palace. It proceeded to the base of the wall, thence it travelled up the wall slowly. The crowd silenced as they saw the circle of light invade the privacy of the palace wall. The circle traveled across the interstices of the bricks, across carved marble pillars, up over the marble protruding balcony until at the parapet, it rested on a pair of hands, a white and purple clothed chest, a garlanded head . . . Nero!

A scream lifted from the crowd.

"It's Nero. Nero".

The light played upon the Emperor's quivering face steadily. The crowd silenced. Nero was screaming at the top of his lungs to the holder of the light, whoever he might be.

"I, Nero, the Divine, am displeased. How dare you to invade my privacy in such an outrageous manner?"

"I, Domitius, sent by Apollo, the god of the sun, have come to eliminate the atrocities that you have caused. I defy you".

"How dare you? Guards . . . guards, seize that boy that I might deal with him in my own manner".

The guards, who had fallen back at the approach of the light, were still too frightened to seize the boy of the sun. Domitius looked at Nero audaciously, and with strong voice acclaimed, "You, Nero, are no longer fit to be Emperor. I have been sent to replace you and set things aright in Rome".

The crowd was yelling hysterically. All this while, the light was playing on the trembling countenance of Nero, but now, if one looked closely, the path of light was not the blue-whiteness that it had been previously, but more of a cream color. The dimming went unnoticed, except to Domitius, who, of course, had no control of this.

Meantime, without noticing the dimming of the light, the crowd had taken up a cry in unison.

"Down with Nero . . . down with Nero". They were screaming all sorts of curses and jibes at him.

He, in the meantime, unable to do anything, stood immovably at the edge of the balcony, staring down in the direction of the origin of light. Now he too noticed that this light was changing color, and though he knew not what this mean, he could tell that the lights was not as strong as it was before.

Domitius began to feel slightly less confident than he had been. The light dimmed to a yellow-tan, a tan, and suddenly the court was aglow only with the faint orange light of the torches that had been moved to the rear to make the sun god's light more effective, and the pale, but ever increasing glow of the same color which was approaching from the western quarter of the city.

The crowd hushed.

Nero screamed at the guards to seize the boy, and looking triumphantly over the heads of the entire crowd, stood on the railing of the balcony and shouted with his head thrown high. "My Divinity is greater than the sun. I am a god and have defeated your puny attempt to overcome me. Disperse, Scum!"

The crowd, screaming in panic, began to evacuate the square, stampeding, running.

Domitius was stranded, held by the guards. He struggled like a madman as Nero came storming out of the front entrance of the palace. Insane with power, he screamed: "Fool, fool of a boy, to try and overcome the divine Nero". He took up a rock and with a glistening, maniacal look in his eyes, brought it down with terrific force on Domitius's head.

In the ever increasing yellow-orange glow from the west one could see Nero lifting, time after time, a rock, and bringing it to rest on the slumped form. His eyes glistened and became more fearful in the orange glow, and the rock came down on the small metal tube that lay on the ground next to Domitius. A tinkle of broken glass was heard through the flame-colored courtyard. A high-pitched screaming laugh lifted high and loud, echoing through the palace, up to the orange heavens. "Sun god, ha, ha, ha . . ."

The sun filtered through the trees with a fiery boldness as Reggie Moore made his way home, as he did each evening after work, up Arrow Street, across Kensington Square, to the small shed that housed the entrance to the Underground. Before descending, to the train, Reggie stopped at the store of a P. Jackson. He went in past the counters of tools and hardware and light bulbs, and up to the man who looked to be the proprietor.

"Good evening to you, sir", said the man, "and what can I do for you?"

"I'd like to purchase a flashlight if I might", said Reggie. "I seem to have misplaced my other one this morning".

"Really, sir, well perhaps Professor Terrence Young, from Oxford found it for you, eh? Ha, ha, ha. . ."

"I say, what the devil are you talking about, and who is this Terr . . . what did you say his name was?"

"Terrence Young, sir. I thought you might have heard. He's that archeology chap from Oxford that was written up in the paper this morning. Seems he was on a safari, no, an expedition, yes, that's what they calls it. Well, anyway, he's on this expedition in Italy to uncover some of the ancient ruins, and what's he find in the ruins of an ancient palace dating back to the first century, somewhere around 64 A.D., . . . a crushed piece of metal that turns out to be a flashlight. And they can't understand how it got there. Seems it was made by a manufacturer in Sussex, and yet, under tests, they find it's been laying under the ruins for 2000 years almost. So maybe Professor Terrence Young found your flashlight eh? Ha . . . ha . . . ha. That'll be six shillings sir. Ha . . . ha".

"By Jove, a flashlight, you say. How the devil did they find a flashlight in the ruins dating back to somewhere around Nero's time, I believe? Oh, here you are, six shillings. Thank you. What paper did you say that was in. I'd like to read about it".

WEEP SOFTLY AND SMILE

The street lights of the little island gleamed and sparkled across the water that separated it from the mainland, like milkwhite pearls on a piece of black velvet. The engine of the car purred with mechanical perfection as the car sped along, across the smooth highway, toward the beach. Lyn was sitting in the passenger seat of the bright red Jaguar, completely thrilled by the thought of riding in Joe Waters' car; his new foreign sports car, too! Joe Waters, the rising new star in popular singing, and Lyn was with him, driving to the beach for a romantic midnight swim.

The car veered off the highway and onto Frederick Avenue, past the parked planes at the airfield, on toward the darkened bridge, lit by road lights and a few blinking red lights at the summit of the expanse. Joe paid the toll and the metal strips of the bridge made a crying sound as the tires passed over them.

Lyn was completely captivated by the entire view. She was looking out of the side window of the car at the sights as seen from a sports car, and yet all the time she could see Joe's reflection in the window. This reflected countenance thrilled her more than all the sights that could be seen from all the sports cars in the world. Joe, a neighborhood boy, making a big name for himself, and he was taking her to the beach for a late night swim. This was about the most thrilling thing that had happened to her in all of her nineteen years. Every girl in the neighborhood would leap at the chance just to be near Joe Waters, the singer.

Joe had always been around the neighborhood, always singing, and bothering people. That's the right word—bothering.

But now came a transformation for him. Now he was making a name for himself in the entertainment field. Now he was a celebrity. His singing was no longer bothersome, but rather pleasing. He was in show business. His little world had expanded to embrace the world of the outside, the world that is open to so few from the neighborhood. Joe was a big man, now. His world extended past the corner hangout, past the street lights, past all the people in the neighborhood, past all those who secretly wished to be more than one of the neighbors; they envied him silently and paid homage to him verbally. He was the most talked about and most boasted about person in the neighborhood.

This transition from local performer to national success was not without its effect upon Joe, who now was displaying a hitherto concealed knowledge of famous people and of facts having to do with the theater. The transition had an effect not only on his knowledge of things but even on his personality. This underwent a remarkable change, for not only was he not an insecure, unsure kid anymore, but now he fashioned himself on his expert appearance and opinion, his judgment and savoir faire.

An instance of this newly acquired knowledge and opinion was when he walked into Sam's soda store on the corner one evening. For years this had been his hangout. The place where he would spend the night, talking to the boys. Leaning against the wall with one leg bent at the knee, foot pressed against the wall, cigarette dangling his thin lips, he would discuss the girls in the neighborhood, or the Dodgers, or the horse races, but now, ah, now this was Joe Waters, the rage of the popular singers, the boy who sold almost a million records with his recording of "I'll Never Let You Know".

He walked into the store in his tapered slacks, no more peg—that was so unsharp—"taper, taper, man, that's the only way to wear them.

Everybody in the 'biz' wears them this way. You know man, like, get hip". Over these conservative pants he wore a quiet shirt with button-down collar. On his feet were thin, Italian styled slip-on shoes.

The commotion, and confusion of the syrup sweet air hushed to a murmured undertone anytime Joe made an appearance—a very rare appearance as a matter of fact. He was too busy to spend much time around the neighborhood these days. He indicated he would sit at the table where his old acquaintances were sitting; a space was quickly made for him; a chair hoisted through the air, and he was seated, to the satisfaction of all the beholding eyes, to his own satisfaction, for everyone was stealing glances at so august a personage, and to the satisfaction of the people he was sitting with, for now they basked in the effulgent light of his illustriousness. After many minutes of awareness, the consciousness of his presence dimmed, and things began to take a more ordinary course. The conversation at his table started to mull over the picture at the Globe, "Gibraltar Affair".

"Yeah, let's go see that, it supposed to be pretty good", said Tommy.

"Naw, whadd-a-ya-kiddin, it's a real lemon. The guy kisses the broad goodbye and sails away, big deal, what do I need to go to the movies to see that. I'll save my money and stay here", said Pete.

Eddie turned to Joe and said, "you seen that pitcha, didn't you Joey? How was it, any good?"

"I caught that flic last week with my agent and I thought it was poor. The acting was unconvincing and the story had a lot of loose ends. On the whole I didn't think it was very good", said Joe in a serious, knowing way. All of this, however, was said in a measured copied way. Not only was the enunciation copied, so was the criticism. What did Joe know about acting or stories, any more than he had six months ago, before he was a singing rage; but now he was accepted as an expert on all things theater, and everyone was impressed by his erudite comments. Joe had been impressed too, when he heard the same words he just mouthed, coming from Sonny Jones, the comic, whom he'd met at his agent's office. Sonny, in turn, may have heard them from someone else.

Tommy, still defending his own opinion maintained that his brother had seen the picture and it was pretty good. Tommy was sitting at the adjacent right side of Joe, at which point Joe swung his head slowly toward the right, tilting it slightly downward, his eyes closed. His head turned past Tommy's position and stopped, a distressed smirk was on his mouth. This was intended to completely dismiss Tommy's idea as ridiculous. Joe opened his eyes, looked at Tommy from the left corner of his eyes and with an uplifted eyebrow and slightly nodding head, said, "Are you trying to tell me now, what a good picture is? I saw it. But you guys go, you'll probably like it".

Tommy was cast down. He looked sheepishly to Joe and said, "I don't want to argue with you, Joe, but my brother liked it. Maybe I'm wrong. Well, what else is there to see, hunh?"

It was forgotten; Joe was right as he turned smugly back toward the center of the group. Wasn't he in on the know?

The darkened road that stretched before the speeding Jaguar was now lit by the lights indicating the guards' gate at the entrance to the private beach. Joe slowed down and flashed a membership card. The guard waved him to enter.

"This is a fancy private place, but a friend of my agent's gave me his pass. Pretty cool, hanh?"

"Yes, I've never been here before. What's it called?", asked Lyn.

"Point Sands".

Lyn sat contentedly viewing the darkened bungalows they passed on their way to the beach. She was still engrossed in the wonderful feeling that overcame her because she was with Joe. She had always liked Joe. He had always been a friend to her, and she to him, even when all others had held him with contempt because he made no money, but only sang; she always cherished his friendship.

Lyn was not an exceptionally beautiful girl, as a matter of fact, the guys in the neighborhood would be moved to call her a nothing, as would Joe, but tonight he felt like going to the beach, and no one else was about, so he asked Lyn. Besides, she probably would go down easier than the other girls because she was a nothing. How could she resist me, he thought to himself. He wasn't in the mood to have to work his points. He wanted someone, not an argument, . . . and Lyn, well, Lyn would do just fine. He pulled the sun visor down, and fixed his hair with the aid of the mirror attached to the underside.

"Watch the car, Joe", screamed Lyn.

"Relax baby", he said as he jerked the car back into its proper lane, "nothing to worry about. I've got everything under control". He pushed the mirror back up and slid his arm over Lyn's shoulder, pulling her gently yet firmly closer to himself. She slid next to him eagerly. She was thinking how wonderful it would be if Joe's interest in her were sincere. She thought she loved him; at any rate, she liked him an awful lot.

The car crunched to a stop on the graveled driveway. Joe turned off the engine, cut the lights, and turned to Lyn.

"Shall we get going?", he asked.

"Mmmhmmm".

They got out and made their way down the beach, over the sand still warm from the heat of the day. The moon in the sky was full, throwing a silvered effect over the small drifting clouds near it. A thin V of light cut its way to the shore over the rippling water.

How romantic, thought Lyn.

Too much friggin' light, thought Joe, *somebody's liable to come along and see us.*

They reached the shore, and Joe spread the blanket so they could sit on it.

Square broad, Joe thought angrily, as Lyn slid her skirt down, revealing the bathing suit she was wearing underneath. Joe started to take his clothes off. *Makes me wear a bathing suit*, he thought. *Oh well, it just takes more time this way.*

"Well, let's get to the water", Joe said as he sprinted away. Lyn followed as quickly as she could.

The surging little slick of water on the beach gave evidence of the coldness of the water. Joe was immersed to his calves in the billowy foam of a wave. "Come on in baby, the water's really fine".

"It's cold, Joe".

"Come on chicken, it's just right", he said as he took her hand in his and ran headlong into the surging surf. The cold water ran over their bodies and they glided through a wave.

"Phagh, phagh", Joe blew the water streaming from his head out of his mouth. "Man this is really cool, in more ways than one, isn't it, baby?" said Joe.

"It's beautiful. I thought it would be much colder than this. I guess it's just the getting in that takes time".

"Yeah, you're right", said Joe with a snickering smile on his face. Lyn got his meaning and also smiled, but in a more reserved and a little embarrassed way.

Joe was right there, all right. Always right at the head of the class when it came to smart sayings or allusions to sex.

A huge wave came stealing in over the darkened water, and broke over the heads of the couple. They were both swept up into the swirling, pounding tiderace; they were thrown down, and over, and carried along with the water toward the shore. The wave spent itself and as they slowed down, Joe felt his legs bump against something. He stopped flowing. His head came out of the water, and he found himself sprawled across a gasping Lyn. "Ha, ha, ha, what a wave", he called out cheerily, although actually frightened.

"Huh, huh", said Lyn, trying to catch her breath. "I thought I was going to drown".

"Come on baby, that little wave didn't scare you did it?" He slipped his arm around her waist and bent toward her for a kiss. She moved not, and as he came closer her arms slipped around him, and they allowed themselves to settle on the moist, runny sand. It was a long kiss, a long passionate kiss, wherein Joe's every effort and movement was calculated to arouse.

"Oh, Joe, I've wanted to be kissed by you for so long", she said when they parted.

"Well, you finally got your big break, eh baby, how was it?"

"Oh, stop kidding around, Joe".

"I'm not kidding baby. I'm as serious as I've ever been in my life", he said as he leaned toward her for another kiss with his whole body. He held her tightly, his body pressed against hers. "Baby, you're driving me crazy", whispered Joe. "I've never had anybody who could kiss like this". He pressed himself on top of her and kissed her again. *Pretty smooth talking, Joey boy*, he thought to himself.

Joe, Joe, if only you meant it, thought Lyn. "Joe, let's go up to the blanket. It's getting cold here on the sand".

"Baby, . . . I'll keep you warm".

"I know, Joe, you're keeping me a little too warm already".

"Ok, let's go up to the blanket", he said, *you rotten little bitch, just when I started to get somewhere*, he thought to himself.

Lyn got a towel from the blanket and started to dry herself.

"Here, let me help you baby", said Joe. He took the towel and started rubbing her back. The towel began to rove over places that couldn't be dried, not through the bathing suit anyway.

"Why not take your suit off so I can dry you all over, baby?"

"No, Joe, I don't want anything like that tonight. Please don't start".

"Why? What's the matter with it baby? It's the most natural thing in the world".

"We're not married Joe, that's what's wrong with it".

"But, baby, you don't have to be married to enjoy life". As he said this he was trying to kiss her neck and shoulders.

Lyn sat up so that she could talk without arousing interruptions. She wanted Joe, sure she did, but not like this. "It's just not right, Joe. It's got to mean something, we're not animals, and besides, just to help you understand it, I don't want to take a chance on having a baby".

"Don't worry about a baby, baby. Ol' Joe'll take care of everything. You know I'm not a square".

"No, Joe, that's all. I think we'd better go".

"Not just yet baby, the night is still so young. It's only one-thirty. What's the hurry?"

"No, hurry, Joe, I just want to go home".

"Sure baby, sure, I only want to please you. I hope you don't get angry, or the wrong impression about me. It's just that you drive me crazy".

"It's okay. Just let's go home. You go ahead up to the car, I'm going behind this dune to change".

"Okay, I'll change on the way up to the car".

Lyn went behind the dune and Joe started up toward the car.

Of all the rotten breaks, he thought as he walked. *I got to get stuck with a goody goody. I thought she'd outgrow that shit. Balls.*

Joe finished changing as Lyn came up to the car.

"All set?", asked Joe.

"Yeah, let's go", said Lyn.

The car churned up the gravel as they sped away from the beach. They both sat in the speeding car without speaking, each to his or her own thoughts. Lyn on the one hand was mixed up. She was crazy about Joe, but she couldn't give herself to him, not just like that. He didn't love her, perhaps he didn't even like her. No, she just couldn't do it. Joe on the other hand was annoyed, affronted, indignant. *Man, I've had better chicks than this for laughs, and she gives me a hard time. So, she's a square.*

The car pulled up in front of Lyn's house with a slight chirp of the wheels stopping.

"Well baby", he said. "I won't be around for a few days, but I'll give you a ring when I get back. I'm looking around in the city for a nice pad".

"A what?"

"A pad, you know, an apartment. Maybe I'll give you a ring Thursday, okay?"

"Sure, Joe, sure".

He leaned over and kissed her, not quite as lustily as before. The wind had been taken from his sail. As he drove away, Joe was furious, and yet there was that challenging element present that made him realize that he would call on Thursday. He was going to have this chick, she wasn't going to put him down. *See you Thursday, you poor duck*, he thought as he drove off.

Thursday arrived and Lyn was in her room, preparing to go down to eat dinner, when the phone rang. *Could it be Joe?* She was hoping fervently that it was, when her mother's voice announced that the phone call was for her. She raced to the phone and picked it up.

Joe's voice filtered through the earpiece. "Hi baby, how's my favorite girl?"

"If that means me", and she hoped it did, "I'm fine. How are you?"

"Cool as ever baby, cool as ever".

"I didn't think you'd call again after the other night", she said. "I thought you were very annoyed because you couldn't get you way".

"Baby, as a matter of fact, I'm very pleased that that happened. I'm really embarrassed about the way I acted, but I respect you so much more because of what you did". *What shit*, thought Joe to himself. "How about going for a drive and a drink with me tonight?"

"Okay, Joe, I'd be very happy to go with you".

"Pick you up at eight-thirty, okay?"

"Fine".

"See you later".

The click of the hanging up of the other end of the line echoed in her ear. She was thinking how wonderful all this was. Joe was now getting to like her a bit. She ran up the stairs and then, just before she got to her room, yelled down to her mother, "I'm not going to eat Mom, I have to get dressed to go out". Then she plunged fully into the task of prettying herself to meet Joe.

The glow of the red and blue lights cast an eerie, even satanic effect on the piano player, as Lyn and Joe sat over drinks in the little spot he took her to that night. He was reserved and yet attentive. His man-of-the-world wise cracking was always with him, but tonight it took on the quality of cuteness, of personality. His mind, however, was active. He had in the forefront of his thoughts, the one, all-consuming thought of making Lyn. It wasn't Lyn so much as it was the fact that he couldn't make her the first time. This to the little man who was becoming a big man, was a fell blow. He was probably too scared to take on the responsibilities of faster women at the moment, so little Lyn had to bear the brunt of his assault. They danced a few dances, and Joe kept up his easy pace of meaningless chatter, meaningless to everyone except the woman who loved him. They started for home around eleven-thirty.

"I wish we could stay out longer, but I have a recording date in the morning. I'll call you tomorrow though, okay?", said Joe.

Lyn was completely thrilled. "Oh yes, Joey, yes. You probably realize this already Joe, but I'm crazy about you. When you called this evening I thought my heart would beat its way right out of my chest".

"Baby, don't talk like that. You make me want to forget I have a session in the morning".

"I wish you didn't, Joey, really I do".

"Maybe we can go out tomorrow night, and make up for the early night tonight, how's that?"

"Sounds wonderful. Call me in the morning".

"Goodnight baby". He leaned over and crushed her willing mouth against his. Their mouths were fused. Their spirits aroused.

"I can't wait until tomorrow night to see you again", she murmured.

"Me neither, chicken—night". *Well, well,* Joe thought to himself as he drove away, *starting to make progress all right. They can't hold you down for long Joey boy.*

Lyn saw Joe again the next night, and this night he was even kinder and more sincere than he had been the night before. He was like a hound dog closing in on the prey. And prey she was, only prey, to be preyed upon. His saccharin sweet talk, the way he held her in his arms, the warm caresses with his mouth upon her ear, were all accompanied by frantic searching thoughts beneath. *where can I take her to do a little balling? I guess I'd better tell her I love her. Hope I don't have her hanging on my neck too long after this*—but on the outside he was wonderful, sweet, warm, Joe.

"Well, let's take off from here, hanh? Let's take a romantic drive to some quiet little spot where we can sit and talk", he said. He paid the check and escorted Lyn out, holding her by the arm. They stepped into the car and slipped out of the city traffic onto the highway.

"Well, you shoulda seen the way the session went today. Five takes were made before the boy in charge picked one. And I'll tell you, it was pretty good, even if I say so. All the guys around the studio told me how good the sound was. Yes sir, make a little room on the top of that ladder boys, 'cause here I come".

"I hope everything turns out well for you, Joe, I really do". She turned front and just watched the road slip quickly and quietly under the car. "Where are we driving to, Joe?"

"Oh, a little spot up the river. It's really nice and quiet and romantic there. Is that okay with you?"

"Fine".

They stopped up on the Hudson, a little shady nook that someone had told Joe about, right near a motel. They sat there, bound in each other's arms for a while, kissing. Lyn was completely given to the moment.

"Baby, I think you're the greatest. Really, I've been with a lot of women before, but you drive me out of at mind", said Joe.

"Joe, I love you".

"I love you too, baby". *Keep shoveling, boy, you've got it made.*

They fell into a passionate embrace which lasted a very long time. At the end of which, Joe whispered to Lyn, "Baby, let's get out of here. Let's go somewhere where we can be alone, and not cramped up like we are in this car".

"Do you really think we should, Joe?"

"Why not darling?", *pour it on now, Joe,* "we love each other, don't we?"

"Yes, Joe, yes, but baby . . ."

"Don't worry baby, just remember that I love you, that's all".

"I'll try, baby. I do love you".

The car chirped off the little clearing and sped down the dark road with the red-tinged glow at the far end of it. That red tinge turned out to be a sign over a building: Motel.

In the days and weeks that followed, Lyn saw little of Joe. Not that she didn't see him around, but he was always quite busy. Busy with the boys, with agents, with sessions, with anything that would give him a good excuse not to see her. She, of course, became somewhat dubious as to their love affair ever blooming into anything further. But it did, much to her regret. The seed in her stomach began blooming into a small Joe and Lyn, she was pregnant. The thought of this frightened her almost into hysteria. Her depression was grave, and with each day that went past, each day that the baby grew, so did her terror. The thought of having a baby out of wedlock, the embarrassment, the shame, . . . oh horrible night that she was mislead by unrequited love. Soon her apprehension took the best of her. She shook herself from her shell, and approached Joe.

"Joe, I . . ."

"Speak up chicken, the big man won't hurt you".

"Joe, it's about what happened that night at the motel".

"Baby, I'm afraid you don't get the idea. I'm not in love with you. It was a mistake. I guess under the influence of the passion. We both fell into something that can never be, that's all. But don't worry, no one will ever know. My lips are . . ."

"Joe, I'm pregnant".

"You're what?"

"Pregnant. It's yours Joe. It's your baby. I guess it was a mistake, but there's more to it now. I'm going to have your baby, Joe".

"Cut the comedy, baby. Joey boy isn't falling for that one".

"I'm not kidding, Joe. I really am pregnant. I just came from the doctor's".

"Well, so you're pregnant, it must be someone else's. When it happens fast, it happens often. I may be fast, but baby we were on the deck before I had a chance to make it safe. I'm not that fast a worker. There must be another cat in the woodpile and you're trying to stick ol' Joe with the price tag. Not today, Josephine".

"You know God damn well there's no one else, Joe, and there never was anyone else either. It's your baby, all right. I can't carry the burden of it alone. I want us to work it out somehow".

"Work it out! Are you kidding? I can't have any kid following me around. I've got my career to think about. I can't get tied down now".

"I think it's a little too late for that now".

"I won't admit it. I'll deny the whole thing. You can't prove it".

"I was talking to the doctor before, and he asked me who the father was. I told him . . ."

"Did you tell him it was me?"

"You are the father, Joe, what else could I say. He said I might have a tough time with you, but if necessary, he would perform a blood test for me to bring to court. Joe, I'm not having this baby alone. I mean that".

"Why you rotten little whore. You think because I went to bed with you once, you own me? Well, you have another think coming, baby, at least one other, and I'm not included in it".

"Joe, it's going to be difficult enough. Don't make it worse".

"Worse, you say worse. Man, my whole career . . . down the drain over a dumb broad and you say things could be worse? Listen, don't do anything crazy. Wait till I give you a ring tomorrow".

In the time between the conversation and the phone call, Joe talked to and asked the advice of about fifteen people. People ranging from the agent of his profession, to the friends of his boyhood.

"How the hell am I going to get that broad off my back? She's just a slut, probably another guy's kid, and I'm going to get tagged with it. You can fix an abortion for $75 in Cuba? What am I going to do? How can I get rid of her? What can I do, what can I do? If I had only used protection. Oh, man, this doesn't happen to me, not Joe Waters. Why I'm just starting up the ladder. She was going to bed with every guy in the neighborhood. Sure, I know Lefty went to bed with her, didn't you, Left? Well, say you did, anyway, hunh? I wish something would happen. Maybe like she fell off the stairs, or something. I can't stand any more of this aggravation. If only I had been smart, I wouldn't have touched that beast". On and on, incessantly, Joe drank, ate, slept, and most of all discussed his problem with anyone who would listen to him. He was frantic. His facade was crumbling. Finally, he screwed up enough courage to call Lyn.

"Hello, Lyn. Joe. Listen, baby, I've been thinking about this baby all night and all day. I don't. know what to do. I'm stuck plain and simple. I can't figure a thing out. What can we do, baby?"

"Joe, I've been thinking about it too, and about what you said to me yesterday, about the way you talked to me. I've decided to tell my mother".

"You told your mother? What did she say?"

"She said that if I married you, or tried to bring you to court, I'd be crazy. On the one hand, I'd only get aggravation, and on the other hand, we'd never be happy. I couldn't live with you, not after what you said".

"Well, then, what can we do? Listen, I can have a guy fix you for a quick, painless, easy abortion. Lots of big people go to this doctor".

"Joe, I won't stand to have a baby of mine killed like that, even if you don't care about it".

"Well, what can we do?", he screamed almost hysterical with fear.

"I'm going away to have my baby, and after I do I'm going to give it up for adoption. So you don't have to worry, you sniveling rat".

"Gee baby, that's a great idea. I'll write to you. I'll give you some money to take the trip with. I'll—"

"Joe, you've given me enough of yourself already. I really couldn't use another thing from you. Goodbye, and I hope I never see you, or hear from you again".

Joe sat with his hand still clenching the telephone receiver, beads of perspiration swelling up on his forehead. "Wow, wow, am I ever lucky. Ha, ha, ha, I'm out of it, and I couldn't be happier. Wow, that was sure close".

It was many months later, when Joe, driving back to the old neighborhood to visit his mother with some theatrical friend, saw Lyn. He stopped the car and got out. She saw Joe, but said nothing.

"Hello baby, how's tricks? How's everything been going for you? I haven't seen you in ages. How've you been?"

"Fine, Joe, just fine, until now. If you'll excuse me, I have more important things to do".

"Sure, baby, sure. Didn't mean to waste your precious time". He looked at his friend to see if he noticed how she avoided him, and got back in the car. "Just some neighborhood hick. She had a mad crush on me, but man, you know how it goes. I had no time to waste on the broad. I put her down real bad, and well, that's the way these little nothings are. They get all broken up about things like that. Come on, let's get to my mother's".

As the big car rolled past, Lyn looked at the diminishing image of what once was something she relished. A smile angled across her face, not a smile of contempt, a smile of pity.

YOUTH, AN ILLUSION

The blue void of the heavens stretched as far as the eye could see. Below, clouds, soft, white, puffy, fantastically soft looking clouds, formed a floor of this solitary world that Rod Lancoval found himself in. The clouds, too, stretched as far as the eye could see, with fragile wisps and arms lifting, curving, and being blown into nothingness, into constantly changing forms, shaped by the wind, ushered by the breezes, aided by the slipstream of the plane. The sun filtered through the canopy of the cockpit brightly, illuminating the dials, wavering with messages for the pilot. Dozens of them, each with its own small purpose for being. Rod pushed his foot against the left rudder pedal, pushed the stick into position, and watched the horizon of cotton tilt toward the right as his plane fell downward toward its mass, through the fog-like haze, and out into the darker realm of the world below, the world that he had left only a few seconds before. He flipped the radio switch and called to the control tower.

"Franco 350 to Teacher, Franco 350 to Teacher, come in Teacher".

"Teacher to Franco 350, come in".

"I'm in position, ready for the run; just give me the word".

"Will start a count. On zero it's your sky. On my mark it will be zero minus thirty seconds. Mark".

Rod checked his watch and saw the seconds until zero tick off.

"Twenty five seconds", the voice from the radio called.

In a few seconds he would begin a 2560 mile race against the clock . . .

"Twenty seconds".

. . . to try and set a new continental speed record.

"Fifteen seconds".

His plane was capable of speed up to 1400 miles an hour . . .

"Ten seconds".

. . . and could travel the entire distance without refueling . . .

"Five seconds . . . four . . . three . . . two . . . one . . . zero . . . Go!"

Rod pushed the throttle to full power. The plane wheeled and headed for the land of sunshine—California.

Up over the coast of New Jersey, Rod looked out to see the outline of the Jersey shore. Through the clouds he could see Atlantic City. *Nice town, Atlantic City*, he thought to himself. He had many a good time there, as he did almost everywhere he went.

Why shouldn't he have a good time, he thought. He could afford it. His Father had made enough money in industrial investments to buy Atlantic City, and Rod, well, Rod knew how to spend money. That is, he did know how to spend before he began to work for Uncle Sam. He had been in the Air Force R.O.T.C. in college, and now Uncle had called him up to serve his tour. The Air Force was good for Rod; it gave him a chance to do something useful for a while, and it gave him a chance to rest up from the hectic way of life he followed as a civilian. Although he'd never admit it, he even liked the service a bit. He had a good assignment, one that he liked. He loved speed, and here he was flying 1200 mph.

Not bad. Right on schedule, he thought. He checked in with the signal tower in McKeesport, Pennsylvania. It was a strange feeling to be flying so fast, . . . so fast that he could beat the sun in a race to California. *Now that's something! Beating the sun to California, or anywhere, for that matter.* Springfield, Illinois signal tower reported clear weather ahead.

Still on schedule, he thought.

His mind began to wander, trying to pass the time, even though it was such a little time, and he had so much to do. He began to think of the speed at which he was travelling. *Took off at 09:06, and I should arrive in two hours. Two hours if I open this plane up, that i'.* He pushed forward against the throttle lever—open full. The air speed indicator edged up to 1350 mph. *Now in two hours it will be 11:00 hours, Eastern Standard Time, but Pacific Time it'll be 08:00 hours. That seems so crazy.* He looked at the chart strapped to his left thigh. "That's what time I'll get there", he said aloud.

Cedar Rapids, Iowa signal tower gives me the same clear weather report. Been up almost an hour. I'm going to make a new record, if everything holds up. Now let's see, if I flew fast enough to beat the sun any place, I'd be flying faster than time, . . . mm, would I? Let's see, from east to west . . . the sun rises in the east, . . . the earth revolves toward the sun, easterly, . . . if I get to a place before the sun, I beat the clock too, . . . right? If I flew to California, as I'm doing now, at a fast enough rate, I'd beat the sun by a couple of hours. I could land, stay on the ground, say two or three hours, or whatever, then take off again, . . . I'd still be ahead of the sun, ahead of time. I could beat time. I could actually beat time! If I could do that, if I could beat the sun around the earth continually, why, . . . why, I could stay ahead of time permanently. And, if time didn't catch up to me, if I kept ahead of time, then maybe I wouldn't age! I could stay young permanently. I could live for eternity, and enjoy myself for hundreds of years. Rod laughed to himself. *I never thought of it quite that way before.*

The mocking smile on his lips disappeared. He became serious, pensive.

The signal tower from Sterling, Colorado barely registered with him. The fantastic—at least up until a few minutes ago it had been fantastic—thought of eternal youth, the secret of staying young could actually be realized through speed.

"Why not? If I can get a plane fast enough I could do it. How fast?" he wondered. "As fast as I can get. And each year I can get a faster one. Yes, of course".

The signal from Tonopah, Nevada hardly penetrated his fiercely calculating thought mechanism. He was close to his destination.

Time: 07:40 hours, PST, he marked on his log.

"I could get the plane I need built in Dad's New Hampshire plant . . . perhaps 2000 miles an hour to start, yes, 2000. That would do it".

The city of Oakland spread out under him like a patch work quilt, greens, and blues, and the reds of brick buildings, the black seams of streets. Just below was the criss-crossed pattern of the air strip.

He called in to the control tower for landing clearance, banked the plane, and was gliding in to a landing. The tires screamed of violation as they hit the run way. All of this was just a hazy dream-like thing now, now that his mind was furiously running through all the opportunities, and possibilities eternal youth would offer him. A band was playing in his honor as he alighted from the plane, but his thoughts were elsewhere. People slapped him on the back, shouting congratulations over the din of the music. He turned from well wisher to well wisher, grinning contrivedly, thanking them. As he passed into the building of the operations office, he looked at the clock on the wall. 7:57 PST.

Time hung very lightly on Rod's hands during the days and weeks that followed his historic flight across the country. He cared little for the time he wasted, or the careless, unimportant things he did. Not as before, when many times he reproached himself for wasting precious time. Life had been so short, and there were so many things he wanted to do . . . But now, now, there was plenty of time, . . . time until the end of the earth, . . . time for everything. His new plane was already under construction in New England, though no one knew it's exact purpose. Just another wild idea of a playboy son. But Rod wasn't fooling this time, this was something serious. He kept thinking of the fun that was in store for him, and of his constant youth.

This entire idea seems to be too ridiculously good to be true, and yet, it is true, eternal youth through speed. I've found the secret of youth. Time will never have a chance to catch up to me. I'll never age. The secret of youth, he howled with joy inside himself. The very thought, the idea of staying young forever moved him considerably. He was completely absorbed in the wonder of it all. He kept repeating to himself, over and over, I can't age, I've found the secret of youth, not only to help himself believe it, but also because he savored every syllable of those two phrases.

When the time came for him to depart from the Air Force, it was with some regret. After all, he was in no hurry to leave his newly made friends, he had plenty of time . . . But yet, he didn't want to capture his youth too late. He wanted to capture his liveliness, his rugged handsomeness . . . no, he had to start now.

Rod made his way to New Hampshire, and stood before the great, sleek plane. His hand tingled as he felt the smooth surface of the ship's skin. What bold adventures they would see together. What shall I call it?, he thought, something very appropriate, hmmm, . . . Venus, the goddess of youth, beauty, gaiety, liveliness. Yes, Venus, she will be my travelling companion.

The silver plane flew over the low, long buildings of the airport trailing a wisp of black exhaust. The powerful sound of the engine sprang over the airfield in its crescendo of percussion, and disappeared, leaving only the void of lesser sounds. As the plane circled into the wind for a landing, two mechanics near the small private hangar Rod rented, looked skyward, traces of pleased grins cracking across their faces. A few feet away, a beautiful young woman, dressed in the expensive clothes of a well-to-do Venezuelan family, stood looking skyward, mixtures of expectation and concern for the safety of her sky man marking her face. As the plane lowered toward the concrete runway, the furrow in her forehead deepened, and as the plane hopped after first touching down, her body started, and her mouth opened in a look of astonishment. Presently her face reclaimed the look of youthful beauty that it had before. The plane was taxiing toward the hangar. The two mechanics ran toward the plane. The beauty just stood where she was and waved vigorously, a happy smile covering her face.

"Welcome back, Senor Lancoval, nice to see you again", said one of the mechanics.

"Hello Miguel, Jose, how're things in Caracas, eh?", he asked as he gave them a slight wink. He jumped off the wing and bounced into a trot, directly into the arms of the waiting girl. "Hello Margarita, how are you", he asked enthusiastically.

"Oh Rod, Rod, it's been so long since you've been here. How long will you stay?" They were in each others arms, hugging and grinning with joy.

"Well, let's see", he said looking at his watch. "It's seven-thirty. I'll stay until one-thirty, how's that? Let's have a crazy time, okay? I don't know when I'll be back again".

"Let's go then", she said, taking his arm, turning toward a waiting car. Rod slipped his arm around her waist and gave her soft flesh a slight pinch. Her body squirmed away from him slightly, and she looked at him in feigned reproach, snuggling closer and smiling into his bright eyes.

The car chirped a bit as Rod drove away in his usual quick way. The two mechanics who were checking the plane, stopped their toil for a moment, and watched the speeding car vanish through the main gate.

"He's one lucky guy, Senor Lancoval. Nice planes, plenty of money, nice girls. All he does is fly from place to place having a good time, . . . and the funny thing is, he never seems to change. I've been here for six years, and he looks the same today as when he flew in here the first time. That was almost six years ago, . . . never changes, . . . just keeps flying and having a good time".

"Wish I had his secret of doing things. I wouldn't mind a girl like Margarita Solina", said the other mechanic. "I bet he has plenty of girls, too. Lucky guy".

And Rod did have plenty of girls. In Hawaii, in Australia, India, France, Japan, . . . everywhere that Rod went, he had girls, and drinks, and fun, and it was true, he never did change. He kept the same appearance, the same smiling outlook on life, never tiring of the mad pace. He surely did have the secret of life.

The plane droned off and soon there was no sound except the solitary squeaking of the closing of the hangar door. Margarita slipped behind the wheel of the car and drove over the moon bathed driveway, out of the airport. Rod circled overhead and then headed his plane westward, a little southward, toward Sydney. He had an appointment there at 7 a.m. He leaned back against the soft cushioned headrest, and closed his eyes. The plane with its automatic guiding devices picked its way across the black sky and over the murky seas below. Rod was smiling to himself. The very thought of his entire life up to this moment from the time he first took off on his secret of youth mission was one, wonderful, happy lark. He had been travelling for six years, and he hadn't aged a day. He was as straight and brisk, and looked the same as the day he started. But his life certainly was different. He had established businesses around the world, made a fortune, and had girls the globe over who loved him. The secret of youth, that's what it was, . . . he had found the secret of youth. *The only reason*, he thought to himself, *no one ever had found it before was they were never able to go as fast as I can now*. His eyes flickered open and he looked at the speed indicator—2800 mph. *Fantastic. And as time goes by, goes by for others that is, his planes would get faster and he would be able to spend more time in each place*. His hand ran across his smoothly shaven cheek, and he felt the youthful vigor there. *The secret of youth*, he smiled. *I've found it. I'll never get old, not as long as I keep flying. I've found the secret of youth. . .the secret of youth. I'll never grow old, never, . . . neve, . . . nev. . . .* His head slumped to the side with wonderful dreams of Sydney in his head. The plane soared on the wings of the air toward Australia.

It was many years later that Rod, while in London, went to a doctor, who had been recommended by a friend, for his semi-annual check-up. Rod actually enjoyed going to doctors' offices; he waited in anticipation for the question he knew would come. "How old are you?" . . . "what, no, it couldn't be". These protestations of disbelief made Rod feel magnificent.

"Well, that completes the check-up, now if you wouldn't mind answering a few questions . . ."

This was it, thought Rod, in gleeful expectation.

"Your legal address is New York, . . . your age is. . .?"

"Forty-five", answered Rod readily.

The doctor looked up, "surely you're joking?", said the doctor.

"Certainly not", said Rod, "Why in God's name should I joke. I have no time to waste. I have a date in forty-five minutes".

Rod really was in a hurry. He had a date with Susan Nystad, the most glamorous model in all of England. Rod could still command the attention of the most glamorous girls in the world. Why shouldn't he? Didn't he look the same as ever. Wasn't he rich, and famous, and of course, young. He had seen glamour blossom and disappear from so many others, and yet he remained untouched by the ravages of time. In appearance, in outlook, in physical stamina, yes he was the same as he had been twelve years before. Exactly the same.

"Pardon me, I didn't hear that last thing you said", Rod said to the doctor, shaking himself from his musing about the past, the future.

"I said, that it isn't possible that a man of forty-five years could be in as good a physical condition as you are. Now, really, how old are you?"

"I am really forty five. You can check that anywhere you like. I am in business throughout the world. I'm sure anyone could confirm my age for you".

"But how, how could this be possible? You have the physique of a young man, a man of say twenty-five, twenty-eight . . ."

"That's right, you see, I have found the secret of youth, the secret of staying young, and have stayed young for a long time".

"The secret of youth?", the doctor asked incredulously. "Could you, or would you, explain this secret to me".

"Certainly", said Rod, "but I must hurry. As I've said, I have a date. Well it was back in the United States, when I was flying a non-stop continental hop for the Air Force. I was flying along, when suddenly I get this brainstorm . . ."

The doctor sat patiently and absorbedly listening to Rod tell of his flight ahead of the sun. He sat in his chair quietly, when Rod finished, and reflected. "You know Mr. Lancoval, that's a very interesting theory you have".

"And a very workable one, I might add, doctor".

"No, I can't see that it's workable, but it is interesting. You see, as well as being a medical doctor, I'm an amateur physicist and astronomer. Interested in all sorts of things, and, well, this theory of yours won't work. It's just not a valid theory". The doctor shook his head. "There is no reason in the world that your theory will work. You haven't really found the secret of youth".

Rod looked the doctor full in the face. The insanity of such a remark. Perhaps the years behind the opened books has dulled this fellow's eyes, thought Rod. Here I am, not four feet away from him, and after twelve years haven't aged a day, and he tells me I'm wrong. I haven't found the secret of youth.

"But don't you think that's absurd", said Rod. "I have stayed young for these past twelve years. How can you say I haven't found the secret of youth. Mind you, not that I haven't heard this before. If I've heard it once, I've heard it a hundred times. In the beginning I was somewhat concerned, but now, after all these years, I am thoroughly convinced I've found the secret of youth. How can you explain my physical and mental state if I haven't".

"Although", the doctor started, "I must say that your state of preservation is marvelous, . . . yes marvelous", he repeated almost to himself, "there is no possible way, under the methods you've been using to beat time. I will admit there is a possibility of beating the earth in its flight around the sun, which is measured in celestial time, that is, time measured according to the interval between a point passing a particular spot in the orbit of another body and its recurrence. In other words, celestial time measures the rotations of the heavenly bodies, but by no means has any effect on physical time. Physical time governs your body, your heart, the mechanisms in your brain, in your stomach. These are made of matter, which will eventually wear out, and then, well the sun will still be in the heavens, and the earth revolving about it, but I doubt if you will still be flying your plane. Don't you see, there are just so many ticks allotted to your heart to beat. The muscles have just so much energy, and then they become weaker and weaker and the last few beats are very slow in coming and then no more. Your body mechanisms are matter, governed by physics, and as such they wear out and you'll die. So as I've said, your state of preservation is marvelous, and I really couldn't say to what you owe that, but your body has definitely been using energy, or aging, all these years. Actually you have only beaten the flight of the earth. You may look young, but I'm sorry to say, you are not. When all the energy is used up, well, you will die as will everyone".

Rod had finished dressing by this time, and was leaving. *This old crackpot doesn't know what he's talking about,* thought Rod. "Well thank you, doctor, your conversation was stimulating, but I'm afraid I think differently".

"That's your privilege, of course. Just think over what I said though. You'll find it makes an awful lot of sense", added the doctor.

And how well Rod knew this, . . . for underneath his calm composure he was thinking of the doctor's words. He got into his car and chirped away from the curb, and lost himself in the city traffic. His mind was working furiously over the principle that the doctor had just expounded. And as he thought of it, his foot imperceptibly eased off the throttle. Presently his car slowed to a stop at the curb. Rod sat there numbed . . . *no secret of youth . . . no secret of youth? I haven't found the secret of youth?* Rod was bent forward over the steering wheel, his head cradled in his hands. Presently, he started the car, and it slowly eased away from the curb, cautiously into traffic. His reflection in the windshield was still young and vigorous, and yet there was a slight bit of a droop to the shoulders, just a slight one.

"I'm getting old, . . . old, . . . can't keep that crazy pace up any more . . . have to watch out for myself. I'm really not so young any more . . ."

WORTH OF A BEING

The ball bounced hollowly from the wall, lifting slowly into the air, then arched downward. Jose skipped backwards, placing himself directly under the ball; he reached his cupped hands upward, and as he stumbled over the curb stone behind him, caught the sphere.

"Yes sir, nice catch, Jose. Let's show them who's boss now", cried Miguel, who was playing the infield on Jose's team. The two teams changed positions, and Carlos, who was also on Jose's team, stepped toward the wall for his turn to be up.

The boys were playing Home Ru, a game played by bouncing a rubber ball against a wall or the steps of a stoop, attempting to get it past their opponents. Each bounce the ball takes on the ground after clearing a measured line away from the wall counts as a base hit, four bounces a home run.

Carlos took a running skip to get more momentum as he approached the wall to throw the ball. He cocked his arm . . .

"Hold it up", shouted a voice from the street which served as the infield, "car coming".

Carlos followed through with his motions, but did not release the ball. He stopped and watched the car slowly pass through the spread-out players, the driver cursing.

"C'mon you little spic bastards, get the frig out of the street".

"Okay, let's go", shouted the players in the infield, disregarding the remark, as the car passed them, disregarding it mainly because they did not understand or speak English very well.

"Whonk", the ball hit the wall, then climbed toward the top of the overspreading canyons of disintegrating mortar with its multitude of grimy window-eyes in which appeared babies, unclothed save for a frayed pair of pants, or men, or women, old and young, with nothing to do except watch a ball reach up toward them and drop slowly down to a pair of waiting hands.

"That's it. Game's over", exulted a voice from the team in the field, as the players, both joyful and sullen, made their way to the stoop on which they always passed the time of day. Each of the boys found a seat, and they sat there and talked about the game, about the girls, or the movies, or anything. People passing on the street, who felt a compelled indignation at the sight of "these" people, would glance toward them and pass on, affecting an air of annoyed consciousness. Little children, dirty and ill dressed, were sitting in the street playing a game with the metal caps from soda bottles that they sneaked out of the top catch-box on the soda cooler in the candy store. The object of the game was to propel the bottle top with a push of a thumb into little chalk drawn boxes on the street, each of which represented a certain amount of points.

Around the corner came Amelio Gonzalez, one of the gang, with a little canvas satchel bag in his hand. He had just come from the gym on Gordon Street where, four or five days a week, he trained to be a boxer. Everyone looked in his direction as he walked over to the stoop smiling. He put his bag down, and joined the conversations. Amelio was proud of his bag, or at least what was in it, his boxing equipment, such as it was a pair of ordinary gym sneakers, a cheap pair of cotton trunks that were white with black stripes on the sides, just like the pros—they made Amelio feel part of the pug game—and some tape that he sneaked out of the gym for the hands. His association with the ring made him a celebrity in his own block, made him feel important, because everyone looked up to the boxer as a man of strength, a man of bravery, an outstanding being.

This idolatry for the pug was no chance occurrence, but could be traced with unerring accuracy throughout the history of fighting. The people involved in the game now, as well as ever before, are those people who are subjected most often to manual, physical labor, those people to whom strength is money, is life, is the means of their existence. To these people the possession of strength is a blessing, and the possession of strength to the degree that is necessary for professional boxing is looked upon with awe. The fighter is revered because he can hit with power, can beat down an opponent in fistic, physical, combat. This man is tough, can protect himself well in the toughness of the society that he has been born into, is respected by the neighbors that he lives with, because they understand well what strength is. Youngsters in these groups grow with the desire and conviction, ingrained, that to be a fighter, to show the world one has strength, will, through the only means at their disposal, prove the worth of their being.

There is also involved in this desire to be a fighter the prospect that with success, through the only means at their disposal, will come relief from this life of drudgery to which so many friends and family find themselves strapped. Physical life is the only reality open to these people and they understand it, and use it, and sometimes die by it. The sharp decline can be noted in aspirants for physical violence in direct proportion to a group that has being more accepted into the realm of economic betterment and the enjoyment of a leisure life. When physical reality and harshness of life has become a memory, so, very often, does the desire to prove one's worth by beating someone else's brains out.

One of the younger fellows picked up Amelio's bag and opened it. He took the boxing trunks out and held them up for all to behold. Lo, the symbol of freedom. The kid slipped the trunks over his pants and began to shadow box, making the forced exhaling sound through his nose that is associated with boxers as they punch. Amelio looked on benevolently, as the master looks down upon his apprentice, tousling the hair of the youngster. All the guys started to cheer, and Amelio, sparred very lightly with the kid.

"Put the trunks on, Amelio. Come on, let's see how they look on you", came the cries from the stoop. Amelio consented and slipped the trunks over his pants and took off his shirt, taking the boxing stance he had seen so many times in newspaper pictures. Everyone cheered, and one of the guys on the stoop got up and in a loud voice, announced, "and in this corner, weighing 145 pounds, wearing white trunks with black stripes, the middleweight champion of the world, Amelio Gonzalez—"

"Yeaaa", a great cheer rang up from the steps, and Amelio danced about at the bottom of the stoop with the boxers bounce, on his toes, from one foot to the other, waving one hand over his head.

It was about six-thirty when Amelio left the stoop and made his way across the street to the stoop in front of his own building. He passed two men who were sitting there talking, opened the door and went in. The usual deep pungent smell that always assailed a stranger's nose, with its acrid oiliness, was undetected by Amelio as he climbed the stairs two by two. This smell was part of his life, he breathed it, ate it, and never knew it existed. He reached the fourth that he sneaked out of the gym landing, walked down the narrow, unlit, peeling plaster, corridor toward the rear of the building.

There were two doors there. He turned the knob of the one on the left and went in. His Mother stood by the kitchen range cooking.

"Mama", he said as he kissed her, then he went into his room to put his bag away. His father was lying in bed, in the middle room, sleeping under a sheet. He had worked all night as a porter in one of the buildings uptown and was getting his weekly day of rest. The front room, which really faced the back of the house, served as Amelio's bedroom, as well as for his two little brothers and a sister. He slid the bag under the bed, and went back to the little kitchen. His Mother was standing there in her faded light green dress, which fell against her sagging bosom and protruding stomach tightly, making great swells in the outline of her body. He sat at the table and began to read the newspaper.

"What time are we going to eat?" he asked. "I'm pretty hungry from all that workout at the gym. Besides I'm going to meet the guys to go to the movies at seven-thirty".

"Your father won't be up before nine", said she. "He worked all night, and he needs one day of rest, but you can eat now, and go out if you want. Maria, Gabriel, come in to have your dinner now".

The two little kids came in and sat down next to Amelio; their mother began to dish out the food. When dinner was over, Amelio washed up, combed his hair, and went out. He ran down the stairs and met the guys in front of the usual stoop. He was the last one to arrive and they all started for the movies. The movie house was about four blocks away. It was a movie house that showed only Spanish pictures because there were so many Spanish-speaking people in the neighborhood. It had once been one of the better theaters in town, but the neighborhood had become less than it was. A big shiny Cadillac car passed the guys and their heads all turned quickly to catch a look at it. Each in his own little secret thoughts said to himself that one day he would have a car like that, and drive around town showing everybody his exhaust.

Yes sir, one of these days soon, thought Amelio, *a yellow convertible*. They reached the movie house and went in.

When the show was over, all the guys made their way home and again sat down on the stoop. They always hung around together, these guys, about twelve of them. They might be considered a gang by people, but really they were only a group of friends, who palled around together. Actually, it was a friendship both voluntary and valuable; valuable since abuse and derision are less hurled to twelve than to one, but nevertheless voluntary because the guys were all close friends.

Presently a patrol car came cruising up the block, and stopped in front of the stoop. Two cops got out, night sticks in hand, and walked over to the gang. One of the cops said, "Okay, let's break it up, let's get going. C'mon move—these little bastards don't even speak English" he commented to his partner. "Boy, if we could only understand what they're gibbering about—probably cursing the hell out of us".

The gang got up and slowly moved toward their houses. "See you tomorrow guys", said Amelio.

It was early the next morning when Amelio arose, shook the sleep out of his eyes, dressed, and started for work. In the kitchen he fixed a small breakfast of bread and jelly for himself, and started for the shop. He worked a few blocks away on the platform of a trucking company. He was treated well there, but there was always an attitude of non-confidence generated by his fellow workers, especially the foreman.

"C'mon Ami", he would say, "let's get that carton over here. No, no, what the hell is the matter with you? Can't you do it the way I told you to, like this—now c'mon—that's better. This kid, you gotta watch him every minute, otherwise he makes a mistake. They haven't got too much brains, these spics". This was the way it went all day, but Amelio was resigned and kept trying to be accepted as a competent worker, an equal, but it was hard. On his lunch break he met Jose, who worked around the corner. They went into the luncheonette, and sat down at the counter. The counterman was waiting on someone else at the other end of the counter.

"Well, how's your work coming?", asked Amelio.

"Ok, but I'm so tired always. I'm going to school for television repair at night. That's why I work so hard over here, so I can make enough money to pay for the course. It's hard though, when I get only thirty dollars a week, and I have a sister and brother to support. School is so expensive, and—hey, don't we get any service in this place", he said loudly, not knowing how else to say what he meant.

"Don't get all excited bud", said the counterman, who was walking toward them. "We've got a lot of people to serve in here beside you, you know. Just keep your shirt on. Whad-a-ya-wan?"

"Give me a baloney sandwich on rye", said Amelio.

"I'll have the same", said Jose.

The counter man walked back to his sandwich board and began talking to one of the customers close by. "Damn spics, all of them are on relief, and they come in here an think they can order you around like you're their servant or somethin'. I wish the hell they'd all go back to their little island and leave us all alone. Here you go, two baloney. That's seventy cents each".

The guys ate their sandwiches, and went out. They stood outside on the sidewalk and smoked a cigarette apiece, and then went back to work.

"See you tonight, Amelio", said Jose.

"Okay, kid, see you later", replied Amelio as he made his way back toward the trucking company platform.

Later that night, when he arrived home for supper, no one was in the apartment. His mother hadn't arrived home from her job yet, she was a seamstress in the Bronx, and his father had already left for his job. Amelio sat down to a light meal he prepared for himself, and went on his way to the gym. As he walked he wished that someday this drudgery could stop for his family, that they could relax and not work so hard. They were always so busy they had no time to be together. His step quickened and his chest swelled. "There's one way to do it", he thought as he reached the steps that led up to the gym. He bounded up two by two, went in and saw Petey standing watching the other fighters. Petey was his trainer, his manager, and his friend.

"All set for a good work out", asked Petey as he came over to Amelio.

"Sure, I'll be changed in a minute".

Amelio came out of the locker room and stepped into the calisthenics corner and began to limber up. Petey came over and began talking to him.

"Listen, kid, if we do all right today, I may be able to line up a fight for you on the east side next week".

"No kiddin', Petey. Who'll I fight?"

"Angel Montez, he's not a tomato can. He's pretty good".

"Just watch me go today, Petey. I'll rip that Angel to pieces". His arms began to flail the air, his mind began to think of the things he could buy with the money he would start to make after he began to fight—a car, nice clothes, money in the pocket. He would show everybody he was worth something. He'd show them.

"Hmps, hmps", his nose snorted, his arms flew, and in his mind he was fighting for the championship of the world, and everyone loved him.

That night when he went out on the stoop to see the guys, they were all involved very deeply in conversation.

"What's up, guys?" he asked.

"We're trying to decide if we should go down to tenth street", said one.

"There are some fights down there tonight, and we are trying to decide if we should go see them", said another.

"Who's fighting?" asked Amelio, "anyone we know?"

"Jose Hernandez is fighting Josh Smith, and Rafael Motara is fighting Angel Montez".

"Angel Montez?" said Amelio in excited curiosity.

"Yeah, why?"

"He's the one I will have my first fight with next week. Let's go down there and see if he is any good".

"OK, Amelio. Let's go guys. We're going to see Amelio's first victim".

"Yes", said the gang collectively as they rose and moved off, down the street. They began to joke, and one of the fellows started a song which they all picked up as they walked along.

The night of the fight came upon Amelio as quickly as he had wanted it to be slow. He sat in the crowded dressing room nervously adjusting and readjusting the tape on his hands. The place smelled a mixture both sweet and pungent of wintergreen, analgesic balm, and perspiration. There were two other fighters in the dressing room both equally nervous as Amelio, and both equally enrapt over the state of their hand tape. Amelio was trying to remember the things that Petey had told him. He tried to remember the way he saw Montez fight that night downtown. "He's fast and shifty, doesn't have much of a punch". His inability to fight was seemingly masked behind a subterfuge of picturesque feinting, ineffectual jabs, and horrible grimaces, which were more menacing that Angel's actual ability to box. And yet, Amelio was nervous. Angel had won three fights before. He had knocked out another fellow on the west side only two weeks before. *Perhaps there was something I missed in his style. No, I couldn't be wrong*, thought Amelio, *that guy can not fight. He's just a pretty picture who has a battle on his hands just keeping from running out of the ring. He thinks he's tough, but it's tougher for him to throw a punch at an opponent than to catch one.* Still there was that doubt. That unreasonable feeling of doubt that crept in through a chink in his stomach armor, It crept in the stomach, and stealthily rose up the trachea, closing off the air passage as he breathed, making the palate work extra hard swallowing. The thought of the defenses and the counter defenses that he and Petey had worked on in preparation for this combat, were now infinitely more complex, more incomprehensible, than they had been at training. *I should have trained more. I'm not even in shape*, thought Amelio. *He'll come in fast. I'll have to push him off, stalk him, hit and stalk, work slowly. Maybe he'll cut me to ribbons. Maybe I won't be able to push him off. If I had only trained more. All the things I have to do! I'll never remember them. Left jab, right cross to the stomach, left hook to the jaw, right upper cut. Ave Maria, I'll never be able to do all those things. He'll either skip away and I won't know what to do, or he'll knock me flat. It's pretty damn easy to feel like a fighter, and even easier to train, but how tough it is to get into that square. I should have stayed home. I'll never even make it to the ring.* That insidious, that underhanded, scheming, creeping, enemy had now invaded his legs. They felt cold, incapable of moving. From far off that silent void of thought he heard the familiar phrasing of his name. He focused his eyes, and there, by the door, was Petey, resplendent in greyishwhite work-out shirt, calling him.

"Come on Amelio, it's time to move to the ring. You fight now".

Amelio hopped off the table. His legs felt as if they were going to buckle underneath him. "Ok, I'm all set", he felt himself saying, although he didn't mean it. He crossed himself and kissed the thumb and bent index finger that formed a cross. Petey helped him on with the gloves and threw an old faded robe that hung in the dressing room for the use of pre-lim fighters over his shoulders.

The roar of the crowd swelled up in his ear, and as he walked down the aisle behind Petey. Amelio felt the eyes of the entire arena on him. They were all looking at him; at least it seemed they were, and they were all looking at him oddly, he thought. They seemed to look at him with humor. They probably knew he couldn't fight well. They were trying not to laugh. Here and there a few people were laughing. *This is terrible*, he thought.

Down by the ringside Amelio met his foreman, to whom he had given two tickets.

"Hiya, Amelio, let's go kid, let's get that guy", said the foreman.

"Yeah, good luck kid", said the man next to the foreman.

That guy with the foreman—he looks awfully familiar, thought Amelio as he slid under the ropes and danced into the ring. The thought of that figure that Amelio could not readily identify roiled his mind tenaciously. *Forget about it*, Amelio said to himself, he had other things to think about at the moment; the fight. He danced into a position from which he could look through the ropes, observed the stranger again.

Of course, thought Amelio, *he's the counter guy at the luncheonette*. He danced around again facing into the center of the ring.

Across the ring he sensed the presence of his adversary. He only sensed, for his attention was very consciously held to a spot on the canvas in front of him. A canvas he felt certain he would be reclining on in short order. With his head still directed downward, his eyes glanced upward and across the roped-in square, to where Angel Montez was warming up. Angel too was looking across the ring, each observed his opponent. Quickly they danced around so as not to look at each other. *Don't want him to think I care one bit*, thought each to himself.

The referee motioned each man to the center of the ring. They stood facing each other, moving their arms back and forth to limber them up. The referee went into the ritual-like speech with the inapt superlative, which is quoted everywhere fight men congregate. Neither paid attention to the words, they were known all too well, and besides, their minds were furiously thinking of all the things that they forgot, or will forget to remember about each other.

". . .and come out fighting", the referee droned.

They touched gloves, went to their corners, and took off their robes.

"Yeahhh, let's go Amelio", shouted the foreman.

"Where do you know that little spic that's fighting from?", asked his friend who sat next to him.

"He works with me over at the platform. You must-a seen him around. He always eats in your place—name's Amelio Gonzalez".

"Oh, yeah, yeah, yeah, I seen him aroun', now that you mention it".

"He's the one who gave me the tickets for tonight", said the foreman.

"No kiddin', first time I heard a spic givin' somethin' away".

"Na, he's awright, this kid. Not like the rest of them. He's awright", repeated the foreman with a shake of his head. "You know, he hasn't much brains—like the rest of them—but he's awright".

"Ah, I don-know. They're all a same far as I'm concerned. Him too. Always bein' smart with their talk—no friggin good".

"Bronggg", the great bell vibrated sonorously.

The two men advanced toward each other, hands extended in front of them. They approached the center of the ring, then began to move to the left in a wide circle, looking at each other's defenses, waiting for the first blow to fall. Amelio swung his hand, which felt as if it were tied to his side. It sailed out into the air and slipped ineffectually past Angel's shoulder. Angel countered with a short underhand left to the midsection, they danced away from each other, and the fight was on. They got into it in one of the corners, arms flailing.

"C'mon, Ami, let's really pour it on. Pretty good fight these spics are putting on, eh Charlie?", said the foreman.

"Yeah, these little spics are pretty peppery. Yow, did you see that left. C'mon kid, again, again. You'd almost think they have guts, hanh?"

The bell ended the round. The crowd buzzed between rounds, although Amelio hardly heard it. Petey was talking to him, rubbing him.

"How-d-ya rate it Charlie. Who d-ya think is winning?" asked the foreman after the second round ended.

"I-don-know. That little spic from your place seems to be doin' okay, but the other guy is doin' pretty good too. I guess I'd call it a draw so far. Yeah, one round apiece".

"Yeah, I guess your right. This'll be the round, the last round".

The bell sounded and the fighters stepped into the middle of the ring, touched gloves and danced away. Amelio had been fighting pretty hard all fight, but he couldn't get rid of the feeling of fear that came into the ring with him. He jabbed out and bent Angel's nose against his face. Angel's right hurtled into Amelio's jaw. Amelio's head snapped to the side, and a quick white flash filled his eyes. He didn't feel the punch too much, but it affected him. He could feel the dull ache in the back of his head increasing. He felt it as a pressure, a blunt pressure that was inside his head. He shot out a left, a right. Montez countered with a short jab, and danced backwards quickly.

If only I could move myself a little, if I could relax, I'd cream this dancer in front of me, thought Amelio as he swung his right against Montez's side. Montez lashed into Amelio with a left hook, a right cross, another left hook, another right cross, a left jab, a right upper cut. Montez was making his spurt. Amelio found himself against the ropes, being hit with all sorts of punches. He saw them come at him. He saw Montez in front of him, grimacing, determined to hit him, his arms swinging. Amelio put his hands up to his face to ward off the punches. Some punches landed, pushing him back into the ropes. He felt the stinging of the landing punches all over his upper body.

"C'mon Ami, dance out-a-there, c'mon", yelled the foreman.

"Looks like your little spic is in trouble", said his friend without looking away from the ring.

"Yeah", said the foreman, also without looking away from the ring.

Amelio felt his knees very weak. He felt like kneeling down, his head was spinning. He could feel the blood surging to his head. He leaned forward into his man, and held on. He was pushed away, into the ropes, and again the rain of blows fell upon him. *I've got to fight him. I've got to. If I don't I'll never get another fight. Got to get going. Got to win*, thought Amelio, visions of his dreams going down to the opposition of an incapable fighter. Amelio moved slow footedly out of the corner. Angel came after him, and led with a left hook. Amelio countered with a hard left hook to the mid-section. Angel was surprised and hurt by the strength of that punch. Amelio, too, was surprised at the strength he put into that punch. He brought a right to Angel's jaw; he fell back. Amelio followed. *Got to win. Santa Maria, help me.* Amelio weaved from side to side. He released a terrific short right to the ribs. Angel felt that punch to the top of his head. Amelio saw his chances brighten. *Cadillac, clothes, money, fame, fortune, easier life for everyone*, punch, punch. His arms were assailing the body of his opponent. Left, right—his arms were going at a terrific pace now, with the precision of a machine, as his body swung from side to side, arms extended, travelling into their mark and out again. He could hardly see his opponent. His determination blinded him. He was so nervous he couldn't remember a thing except to keep throwing punches. Angel was against the ropes. Amelio's arms were going without his controlling them. Left, right, left, right, right. The crowd was on it's feet, roaring,

Got to get him, got to, go down, you bastard, go down. Amelio's arms didn't want to move. It was difficult to get them to fly forward. They were stiff from over use, but he forced them forward, left, right, left, right—

"Brongg", he heard the bell, a loud roar, and found himself hanging on the shoulders of the referee and Angel.

"Nice fight Angel".

Angel, who had suffered from that last barrage of punches, nodded and clung to his seconds who had come into the ring.

"That kid really showed him a thing or two didn't he, Charlie?"

"Yeah", Charlie was saying, nodding, a pleased smile on his face. "That kid that works with you is all right. You know that?—he's okay. What did you say his name was?"

"Amelio Gonzalez. Told you he was awright".

"Kid is a good little fighter. Real good. Why don-t'cha bring him over Monday, the lunch is on me. Amelio Gonzalez hanh? Pretty good! Yeahhh, nice fight Amelio, nice fight kid", yelled Charlie, who was on his feet with the rest of the crowd, yelling loudly in tribute, as the referee raised Amelio's hand aloft, toward the smoke filled top of the arena.

ANNUS MIRABILIS

The pure, shining white, death colored, bleached, disinfected squares of the wall tiles with the light green color of the upper wall overhanging, stared silently, opaquely, blankly back at Bob as he lay listlessly, bleary-eyed on the bed. The white uniformed people hovering about the clean white beds in the long hall, upon which males of all ages were prostrate with pain, scurried back and forth with soundless speed. Just the rustle of a nurse's silken slip underneath her uniform, could be heard once in a while, . . . but this was not disconcerting. It made one feel that there were joys in life yet to be encountered, and perhaps it would be better not to die—not here anyway—not now—not in this whited sepulcher full of diseased, dead, or dying, rotten bones and flesh.

Bob reached his hand down along his blanket enclosed side until it struck the even smoothness of the newspaper that was lying on the bed. His hand just lay on top of the daily newspaper, resting, waiting until he had enough strength to pull that paper up to where he could read it. Summoning all his nerve and strength and setting his teeth hard against each other, he swallowed. The swollen uvula in his throat, that damn silly piece of flesh hanging swollenly from his palate, rode forward and back on his swollen tongue as if a hand full of sand was stuffed in his mouth.

"Oh Jesus Christ, Jesus, Jesus Christ, please . . . I can't stand this another minute", Bob screamed within himself in uncontrollable delirium of imagined discomfort. "Please, please . . . can't you let this go away. It's only a silly little swelling . . . What are you trying to do to me? Why don't you help me? Why don't you do something?"

That little uvula that was making him choke and gag was wearing him down. He picked his head off the pillow slowly and propped the pillow behind his head with one hand as he pulled the newspaper closer to himself to read it. The cool air away from the warm unmoving air of the pillow stung his ear and he winced with pain.

"Madonna mia, . . . Madonna mia, . . . please", he prayed in Italian, but even the God of his people's language did nothing to relieve his pain.

"Nurse . . . nurse", he called out to no nurse in particular.

A white frocked girl of about twenty years came over to his bedside, looking down into his face with an innocent youthfulness that had become callous through exposure to grief. "What is it now, Mr. Campanella?"

"Nurse, . . . my ear, my throat, my back, my head, . . . everything . . . Can't you do something? I can't stand it. Tell the doctor to kill me. . . give me some dope . . . anything. Just get rid of this damn silly swelling . . ."

"You'll just have to be patient, Mr. Campanella", she said, impatient with his complaint. "After all, it took some time for you to get what you've got. It won't go away in two days".

"Three days. I've been in bed three days!" She shrugged phlegmatically. "Let me go home . . . Let me kill myself . . . something. I haven't got time for this . . . I haven't the patience . . ."

"Don't be such a baby. You've got little more than a sore throat. Look at the others. They're a lot worse off than you, and they don't complain half as much".

"I know, I know", he said dejectedly, feeling guilty as he looked about at the others on the beds.

One old man, cadaverous looking, his head like a skull with a bit of skin stretched over it, his eyes sunk way back in his head, lay in the unshadowed room on the iron bed, just staring at the ceiling, never moving his glassy eyes from above. His tiny, thin figure pushed up an insignificant bump under the sheet. Next to him was a younger man, a little older than Bob, whose face was turned toward Bob, only it didn't see him . . . His mouth kept opening and closing in spasm, as his eyes rolled uncontrollably from side to side

"Nois . . . nois", the man kept calling. From time to time a nurse would pull the covers over him and leave.

Right next to Bob was a fellow who looked normal and healthy as his figure emerged over the sheets, but underneath, where his midsection should be, a huge watermelon pushed up the covers . . . only it wasn't a watermelon, it was him, . . . and he didn't say a word.

A scream echoed from the end of the corridor and Bob twisted around suddenly to see what had happened. A nurse ran over to a man on a bed as he twisted and contorted, writhing with pain. "Stop it . . . Stop it", he screamed pathetically with the full strength of his weak body . . . "Christ help me".

Bob lay his head back on the pillow resignedly and looked up at the ceiling, trying to rest and not complain. Actually it didn't hurt much . . . not really. It was the inconvenience . . . the botheration . . . the being in bed for three days . . . the impossibility of swallowing without pain that was so vexing, so annoying . . . the utter feeling of hopelessness and dejection. He leaned over and spit the excess saliva from his mouth, and it splattered metallically into a little pan by the side of his bed . . . this saved him from swallowing all the saliva that now purposely found its way to his mouth just to add to the annoyance.

"If only they could give me something to take this little swelling away, a shot of something, I'd be all right".

"Have to take your temperature now, Mr. Campanella", said a nurse as she stood over him next to the bed.

"Okay".

She put the thermometer in his mouth.

"Leimmn . . . himm, I mn". He removed the thermometer. "Listen, just get me something to get rid of this swelling . . .".

"Your temperature! Would you put the thermometer back".

"All right, all right, but get something. Why the hell do I have to suffer at all? Am I supposed to enjoy this pain cause it's not as bad as those guys". He nodded toward the rest of the ward.

"I'll talk to the doctor", said the nurse as she watched him put the thermometer back in his mouth.

Bob lay back on the pillow and picked up the paper and began to re-read for the fortieth time the day's news. "Tuesday, April 29, 1958 . . . Navy fails to orbit fourth U.S. moon . . . it was jettisoned into Atlantic ocean about 1400 miles out and blew up . . . about 18,000 miles an hour speed".

The nurse took the thermometer out of his mouth and studied it. "Just look at that", she said pointing to an article in the paper next to the column about the satellite. *Arm Removed. Stritch Makes Good Progress . . . for weeks the Cardinal felt severe pain . . . all treatment failed to relieve the thrombosis . . . arm amputated above the right elbow . . .*

"At least you're still in one piece", she said.

"Yeah, . . . maybe I can make a flight to the moon soon".

The nurse marked his temperature in his medical chart and walked back to her desk. A young doctor, probably an intern, who had been assigned to the ward since Bob was there, walked in, looking at each patient as he passed his bed.

"Hey Doc", called Bob in a world weary, low voice . . . can't you just take this swelling away so I can go home".

"Take it easy", urged the doctor. "It'll go away in a day or so, maybe tomorrow you'll be all right. You know, you're not a machine. I can't take one part out and put another in. I have to work with what you've got".

"But there must be something . . . I gotta suffer like this with a silly God damn swelling . . . Give me something just to take it away".

"If I had something I'd give it to you, believe me. Here, read your paper".

"I read it a hundred times".

"Well here's a 'News'. You finished with this, Joe?" the doctor asked the patient with the watermelon of a stomach.

The fellow just rolled his eyes toward the doctor and nodded his head slowly. His eyes skimmed quickly over Bob, smiling vaguely, as they unfocused and searched the vast darkness of resignation overhead for an answer.

The doctor handed Bob the paper and walked down the aisle toward another patient.

Bob read the same news in 'The News' . . . an item he hadn't seen. *British explode a clean bomb . . . a nuclear device believed to be a clean hydrogen bomb, designed for low radio-active fall out . . . fall out was negligible.*

"How great", thought Bob, gritting his teeth and swallowing again . . . pain pulsed through his body and he let the paper fall on his torso as he lay back on the pillow. "How great . . . how magnificent . . . how benign. They worry about you being sterile while they blow you to bits". He picked up his head and looked around the room again. All the rest of the men were still lying in their nice white clean hospital beds, waiting for relief.

A NORMAL, MODERN BOY

The round cornered square of light flickered and glowed with the shadowed flora and design of the electronic wonder of the world. Little men were riding little horses across a miniature world of sand and cactus. Puffs of smoke issued from miniature firearms in their hands; one of the little men fell off his little horse, rolled in the dust, over and over, down a steep hill, over a cliff, dropping rapidly toward water below. A long dark shadow was thrown over the buzzing electronic world which slipped upward once in a while only to be replaced after a short interlude of lines by another exact copy of itself. The long, dark shadow moved across and down the square of light, completely hiding the little man who had, by this time, reached the end of his ethereal descent and had now taken a watery exit from the minute world. The shadow twisted almost imperceptibly, and the little world was thrown into an obscurity of dull grey-black nothingness, with only a pin point of light in the center.

"Aww, why-d-ya turn the television off for, Daddy?" said a completely crushed voice from the shadowy rear of the room.

Frank Heron looked, nay searched, into the umbrageous depths of the room and said, "Jim" . . . his voice cracked; he cleared his throat and began again. "Jim" . . . Frank was nervous. This time he was going through with it. How many times before had he resolved to talk to him, to take Jim in hand and speak to him, father to son; to get to know Jim with that closeness that he had known with his father. He wanted to be a pal to his boy, and now was the time, he thought, now was the time he should talk to Jim. Jim was old enough now to be spoken to . . . but it was so difficult to start. He reached for the TV program guide on the top of the television set and began to dog-ear the pages.

"Jim, I want to walk with you . . . where the devil is the light in here? I can't see a thing. Jim, are you still there? Where are you?"

"Frank . . . Frank, would you come here a minute", called Mary, Frank's wife, who was in another room.

Frank went out of the television room—it was the room that had been his den, B.T., that is, Before Television. But now it was the television room. He found Mary in the kitchen soothing the spectacle of a weeping Jim, who had run to his Mummy when Daddy had turned off the television. Well, it wasn't his fault that he was on the road so much with business; it wasn't his fault that the child had become so attached to his mother—but, damn if it didn't peeve him when the boy would run crying to his mother about what daddy did. And it peeved him even more when Mary would say:

"Now, Frank, you know you shouldn't upset Jim so. After all, you don't want to give him a complex, do you? You know what the doctor said—don't restrain the child, it shows up in after-life in the form of grave neurosis. Do you want that for your son? After all, Frank, he only wants to watch his favorite programs".

"May, darling, you know I don't want to frustrate, or oppress, or restrain, or retard the boy in any way what so ever. I only wanted to talk to him, to become more friendly with him. I was going to suggest that he and I take a walk together, that's all. There's nothing oppressive with that, is there?" he asked, not knowing if there was.

Mary smiled, turned to the clock on the wall, then to Jim. "Would you like to go for a walk with Daddy, dear? The program is over now, anyway, and it would be very good for you to go out and get some fresh air".

Jim was reluctant, but with a smile from mother, and a promise that she would watch the seven o'clock show with him, Jim agreed to go for a walk with Daddy.

"Now go get your coat, and you and Daddy get a nice walk before we watch Captain Smasheroo, alright?"

Jim waddled out of the room with that odd side to side gait that obesity necessitates. The boy had been rather lean in his early stages, but lately he had put on a great deal of weight. So much so, that Frank had been worried and brought him to the doctor; a bit heavy, the doctor said; there was nothing physically wrong with Jim, just the need of a little dieting, that's all. Thank heavens. Jim was their only child. Now Jim and his mother dieted together, which sort of bonded them even closer together.

"Oh, Frank, Frank, it's so good of you to suggest to take Jim for a walk", said Mary as she watched Jim waddle out of the room with a mixture of pity for his struggle to move, and love for her only child. "This will sort of allay any fears that he has of you. Oh, you know, not that he fears you. But he hardly ever sees you, and might be a little nervous when he's with you. This will be wonderful for his psychologically, just wonderful", she said as Jim came into the room with his coat on.

"All set to go, Jim?" said Frank with a contrived smile playing on his lips. "Let's go and see what's new and beautiful in the world, shall we?"

The Fall sunset was reflecting off the buildings of the stores on Main Street brilliantly, as Frank and Jim walked along the street looking in the windows. It was hard to see into the store windows because of the sun. Frank and Jim would lean against the window, hands cupped to the side of their eyes to cut the glare, then walk on, leaving the print of the side of the hands on the windows.

"Well, how are you doing with your school work?" Frank asked Jim in a very man to man way.

"Oh, fine, Dad, fine. I got my report card in the mail yesterday. I had three Cs and a B".

"Say, that's not bad", said Frank; after all, he didn't want to frustrate the boy. "How did your lessons go today?" Frank asked after a silence that became oppressive. "Did you learn anything new?" he said, trying to allay the boy's fear of him.

"Well, I was doing pretty good the first fifteen minutes, but then the vertical hold on the set went kapooee, and I missed my entire arithmetic lesson for the day and half the geography, and then the Billy Kramer show went on, and I never miss the Billy Kramer show . . . so my lessons didn't go so well today".

"Well we'll get the set fixed for tomorrow, so you can get a good day of lessons in. But I don't understand Billy Kramer in the middle of your lessons. Didn't Mother make you put your lessons back on?"

"Nah, but that's okay. Thursdays and Fridays are repeat days anyway. They put Monday's, Tuesday's and Wednesday's lessons off for those who missed them, so I'll see what I missed Thursday. You don't have to worry about the set being fixed though. Mom called the man to fix it already. Captain Smasheroo is on tonight. We couldn't miss that".

"Yeah, that's right—Captain Smasheroo. Wouldn't want to miss that", Frank said bewilderedly. He looked at his watch. "We'd better head back home if we want to catch the beginning of Captain Smasheroo", he said, just to show the boy they had something in common.

As they walked along, Jim pointed toward the big elm tree that had been Frank's favorite haunt when he was a boy and had lived on this side of town.

"What is that, Daddy?" asked Jim.

"What is what?" asked Frank, looking ahead for what Jim was looking at.

"That", said Jim, pointing straight ahead, down the street.

Frank looked, stared, strained, craned, moved his head from side to side, tried to focus on the same plane as Jim, but could see nothing.

"What, where, Jim? Show me what you want to know", said Frank, pleased, feeling that, at last, he could get to a closer feeling with his son by being able to explain things for him.

"This", said Jim, putting a pudgy finger on the trunk of the elm.

"This?" rasped Frank. His voice cracked with incredulity and surprise. He cleared his throat and asked again. "This?"

"Yes, this, this", announced Jim, striking the bark with his pudgy finger again.

"Why this is, why this is . . . it's a tree . . . an elm tree". Frank was speechless. Could it be the boy had never seen a tree before?

"Oh, I never saw one so big before. They're usually smaller than this, aren't they Daddy?"

"Why, no, Jim. They grow in all sizes", said Frank, somewhat relieve at this answer to his unasked question.

"I never saw one this big . . . all the ones I saw were small".

Frank wondered, but said nothing. As they walked as briskly as Jim could manage back to the house, Frank espied a long, wide verdant field; the same field upon which the bonds of closeness and friendship between he and his father were sealed during numerous 'catches' with a football.

"Say", said Frank, inspired. "How about, when Captain Smasheroo is over, we come over here with the football and have a catch. You still have that football I gave you for Christmas a couple of years ago, don't you?"

"Yeah, I have it, but I don't want to play football, Dad. There's the Pabst Beer Variety show on right after Captain Smasheroo".

"Well, what the heck. I don't see you very often, and missing one program won't kill you, will it?"

"I don't play football anyway, Dad".

"Why, what's the matter with football. Don't you like it?"

"Well, it's not that I don't like it", said Jim. "I like to watch it, but I've never played it. I don't know how. I mean, I know how, but I just never have".

"You've never played football?" asked Frank astonished. "Don't you ever go out with your friends and have a catch?"

"Well, I don't have too many friends in the block, anyway, Dad".

"You've got to cultivate friends. You have to give and take. You just can't expect people to bow down to you, you know".

"Yeah, I know", said Jim. "But it's not that. It's just that, well, I hardly ever see anybody my own age. They don't go out much either. They don't go out and play ball, not very much, anyway. Once in a while they do, but I don't know any of them, and I don't feel like playing ball anyway".

Frank scanned the ball-field, remembering his father throwing the ball to him, running . . . but Frank's dreams of renewing ties like that had just been crushed, beaten, out trendexed by electronics. He hunched his shoulders and kept walking.

"Dad".

"What, Jim?", said Frank without even turning.

"This is grass out here, isn't it? I mean, well, is grass always this color, or is it different colors? I never saw colored grass like this before".

"You never saw colored grass before. What did you think it was, anyway?" asked Frank.

"I don't know. It's always dark grey on the television. We don't have a color set, so I never knew what color it was".

"Well, grass is always green, all right", Frank said in an exasperated way—"oh, oh", Frank said to himself, "shouldn't lose my temper. Mary would be angry and Jim will get a complex".

As it was, Jim was not walking with Frank any more. He was still standing in the spot on which he was when Frank issued those angry words. It seemed as if the first angry words Jim ever hear riveted him to the spot where he stood, head down, sulking . . .

"Oh, come on, Jim. I didn't mean it", supplicated Frank as he walked back to where Jim was standing. "Captain Smasheroo will be going on in a few minutes. Let's hurry".

Jim moved, not from love, not from love of Frank, that is, only a desire to see the Captain.

When they arrived home, Frank asked Mary to stand outside the television room.

"What is it, Frank, come on, Captain Smasheroo is going on now, and you know I promised Jim . . ."

"Mary, do you think that this television school that Jim watches is doing him any good? I mean—?

"Shh, don't say things like that so loud. What the matter with you? Of course it's doing him good. Didn't you see his report card. We got it in the mail yesterday", whispered Mary.

"Yes, I know, but what's the matter with the boy?" Frank whispered back.

"Nothing, nothing at all is the matter with the boy! He's a perfectly healthy, normal boy. You didn't say anything like that to him, did you? I mean, even imply that there was something wrong with him?"

"No, or course not", answered Frank.

"Well, good thing. You know what something like that could do to him".

"Yes, I know, but I can't understand what's wrong with the boy. I mean, we were walking and he didn't even know what a tree was, or how to play catch, or even what color grass was. All he knows is television. When I was a boy I used to climb in the very tree he asked me about, and we had a football team, and . . . well, he, he . . ."

"Shh, be more quiet. Do you want Jim to hear you?" cautioned Mary.

"Well, he", whispered Frank as quietly as he could, "he didn't even know what these things were when he encountered them in the street".

"Frank, when you were a boy, things were different than they are now. You must understand—things have changed. Jim is a perfectly normal, modern young man".

"Oh, come, will you. Don't you see, this watching television all the time and the catering to him isn't doing him any good. He's got to grow up sometime and face the world".

"Don't expect too much too soon out of the boy", whispered Mary. "After all, if you rush him, you may leave a scar on his unconscious for the rest of his life".

"But, Mary, the boy didn't even know a tree", said Frank, exasperated.

"That's all right, he will. Don't worry. If only you don't rush him. Believe me, Frank, I know. I'm his mother. And the doctor assured me, he's perfectly normal, so there's nothing to worry about".

"Nothing to worry about? Perfectly normal? For Christ's sake, Mary", shouted Frank at the top of his lungs, "that kid is eighteen years old!"

A GENTLEMEN'S WAGER

The blue-grey wisps of smoke curled upward, and then slowly drifted toward the window. They squirmed through the small opening at the top, which was left to assure the passage of fresh air into the office, and flew out over the interminable, eternal, huddling of the mortar subjects of the goddess New York. Large buildings, small buildings, dimly lit ones, neon emblazoned ones, all sat and huddled together for extra warmth, while without, the humans were walking faster to stay warm. Small spumes of steam emitted from their mouths as they rushed toward Broadway, or down to Rector Street, or over to Wall Street, or Greenwich Street.

"It'll probably be colder than all kinds of hell, on the island tonight", said Frank, his shoulder against the window frame, watching the insect-sized people spuming steam and scampering into the innards of the silent building entrances far below.

"Don't let that worry you", replied Jim, who was across the room, bending over the small cabinet bar that he had built into his office for convenience sake.

"C'mon, let me have that glass of yours, so I can freshen it. This damn bottle of scotch has been here almost a week . . . you want it to go sour?"

"You must wrap yourself in your money when you get home", said Frank, chuckling, "that's why you're so much warmer than I am. You have so much more of it than I do".

"Now come on, Frank. I know damn well you've been doing quite well yourself lately. Why, just yesterday, Henderson was telling me that that Helicon Mountain deal of yours made quite a nice bundle. You're not fooling me, Frank. You must keep pretty warm in that house of yours, too".

"Sure, Helicon Mountain went fine", said Frank, "but did you hear about the fiasco of that Quatrain Supply? I lost my shirt".

"Let's not talk any more business now", said Jim with a wave of his hand. "I'm pretty tired from all battling and trading today. Give me your glass, and let me get you another drink so we can just relax and not go on with all this nonsense".

Frank handed Jim his glass. He remained at the window, looking across the room at the wide expanse of fine wool worsted that covered Jim's broad back. Jim . . . James A. Ackland to be sure, most successful of the securities traders in the neighborhood of Wall Street. "Why the hell should he worry about a little loss or gain, . . . he's worth millions to begin with. Just a drop in the bucket to him", thought Frank, Francis R. Graham, to be sure, who was one of the most successful new-comers to the market.

Though it was never discussed broadly or openly, it was fairly common knowledge to those of the inner groups on the Street, that Jim had given Frank his start, had taken him into the fold when Frank began to invest, had guided him and helped him build up his holdings through loans and advice. Jim had done quite a lot for Frank, and yet, well, maybe that was the reason for the hidden vexation, the never voiced resentment that Frank hid deep within himself. Perhaps it was that Jim had been too helpful, that Frank was too much indebted to him, that caused him to what—resent Jim? Not openly, not boldly, for he still needed Jim—but quietly, covered over by a devotion, hidden by a desire to be near Jim, to be like Jim, to bask in the effulgence of success.

Frank wanted to be like Jim; look at the money that Jim had, that fabulous pile, compared to Frank's small nest egg, that was added to only by the diligent, constant, restless toil of his cunning brain, . . . while Jim merely had to breathe on or near a transaction, just suggest that he was interested in a property, and lo, the heavens and earth trembled and a pot of gold was ushered to his feet. The only effort necessary on Jim's part was to stoop over and pick it up.

Perhaps Frank envied Jim's power of . . . but hadn't it always been this way, even when they were in college?

"Say, Jim", Frank said once when they were living in the same dorm. "I was wondering if you might be able to help me out. I've sort of goofed my date for the week-end and now I'm stuck. Do you think you might be able to help me out with a number I could call?"

"Sure thing, buddy boy", said Jim. "Just let me get to my room and I'll see if I can hunt up a number for you". And he did. Jim could always do anything, get anything, be anything he wanted, while Frank had to toil relentlessly, had to snivel and cringe while Jim merely had to breathe.

"Here you are, buddy boy, another drink to help keep you and your money warm?", said Jim jokingly.

Frank took the drink, lifted it in salutation, and drank deeply, watching Jim out of the side of his eyes. Jim stood staring back at him.

"What are you staring at? Is there anything wrong?" asked Frank, lowering his glass.

"Hell, no. Just thinking of all the things that you and I have been through together, college, the war, then when you returned from the coast. It's been a long time that we've been together, hasn't it?"

"You're right. It has been a long time. And you've been damn good to me, damn good. And don't think I don't appreciate it. Why without you, I'd still be selling textiles. Yep, I owe everything I own, everything, to you and your help. I owe you plenty", said Frank with narrowing eyes as he raised his drink again.

"Say, look at this paper", said Jim, leaning with one hand on the conference table that dominated the side of his office, looking at the early edition of the Journal. Frank lowered his drink and moved to the table to see the paper.

There on the front page was the full length picture of an assassinated man shot down in the street the night before, assailant unknown. The detailed story leaped off the pages as Jim read, Frank listened, until he finished the article.

"This town is getting pretty bad", said Jim, looking up from the printed page. "I tell you, it's almost as bad as Chicago in the Prohibition days. I'd be afraid to walk down a street in town at night, afraid I'd be mugged, or beaten, or even murdered", said Jim.

"Well, it's not as bad as Chicago and all that. I mean, after all, in it's heyday Chicago had about five hundred gang killings, and hardly any of the killers were apprehended. I mean it hasn't gotten to that stage yet", replied Frank.

"It's bad enough, Frank. Pray God it doesn't get as bad as that. Five hundred killings. And hardly a murder solved. Boy, that's just crazy", said Jim, hitting his palm on the conference table. "The police were probably bribed and all that, but still, five hundred killings. That's a hell of a lot".

"It sure is . . . five hundred", said Frank reflectively.

"And hardly any solved", continued Jim.

"I'll admit that there could be a perfect murder committed, but those things in Chicago weren't perfect murders. You can bet on that".

"You really think a perfect murder could be committed, Jim?"

"Certainly. Take all the proper precautions, the right steps, and you could kill someone, anyone, and no one would ever find out. It probably would be easy".

"You're kidding. You really think you could set up a perfect murder. I mean really, not only idle thought?" said Frank, genuinely interested, struck, seemingly, by a flying, glowing spark. Jim, who had been taking a sip of his drink, stopped, put down the drink, and looked at Frank.

"Well, yes. I honestly believe I could. If I wanted to. If I put my mind to it, I'm sure I could".

"I don't believe you could do it", said Frank, shaking his head. "Nope, I don't believe it".

"Well, I don't know if I want to prove it to you, or not, but I sure as hell know I could. I've thought about it before. Not doing it, or course, but just the idea, the method, and I thought of a plan that I know could work if I developed it a bit more".

"Aww, that's a lot of nonsense. You'd be picked up in twenty four hours and slammed in the chair if you ever tried it. I know you, and all that confidence you have in yourself, how you think everything is a challenge and you have to stand up to it, but this time you're just blowing your own whistle. I'd damn near bet you anything I own that you couldn't do it".

"I'll be God damned. You telling me I'm a blowhard?" stammered Jim, his jaw set grim and hard.

"No, I'm not calling you a blowhard. I just say you're blowing your own whistle this time. You couldn't do it in a million years, and I don't care what you say", said Frank purposely.

"You're telling me I don't know what I'm talking about, eh? I'll take you up on that offer of yours. If you can put up enough capital, I'll show you who's blowing his own whistle. Come on, what're you willing to wager?"

"I don't mean for you to do anything crazy".

"Let's go, how much do you want to be me. C'mon, let's go", said Jim, in a determined, impatient way.

"All right, if you're really serious, how about a thousand?" replied Frank.

"Make it serious money, Buddy Boy . . .".

Buddy Boy, that damned name. How Frank hated it when Jim called him that.

". . . you can do a lot better than that, can't you?" continued Jim.

"Okay, make it ten thousand".

"That's getting better. If you make it fifty thousand, I'll take it", said Jim.

"Jesus, don't go hog wild with these figures, Jim. After all, I don't have the kind of money you have".

"If you've got fifty thousand to bet, we've got a deal, put it up, Buddy Boy, or forget it".

"You've got it", snapped Frank with irate rapidity. "Fifty thousand that you can't put together a perfect murder".

Jim and Frank shook hands to complete their gentlemen's wager. Jim briskly put his drink down and in serious, almost deadly, manner, took his overcoat off the hanger and put it on his back. Frank looked at him in an astonished, dumbfounded, and yet, unobservedly, pleased way. Jim turned to Frank and said: "are you coming, or do you want to take the train home?"

"No, wait a minute", said Frank. "I'll be right with you. Just let me get my coat out of my office. You go ahead down and warm the car. I'll be down in a second".

The steel cables that were suspended between the struts of the bridge swept down from the great heights, and then soared upwards again, as the car rolled forward, past strip after strip, beam after beam, girder after girder, of mute, dark, steel. Jim was driving across the bridge at an unusually slow pace this evening, obviously occupied with the thoughts of the foul negotiation he had just been a partner to. Below, the murky water jumped and quivered like a gelatinous mass. The lights of the shipyard shone forth and reflected off the water, making weird, vari-patterned designs of abstract lights thereon.

Jim spoke from the somber depths of his being. "Frank, tomorrow, you bring in the amount we've agreed upon. By then, I think I'll be able to lay the groundwork for a scheme, . . . but don't let anyone know about the money, otherwise, we'll arouse suspicion from the start". Then he pressed his lips in a determined, familiar twist, one that Frank had seen so often before. It was a horrifying evil smirk now. Some time ago it had been an amiable grin, . . . and before that, it had been a sign of conviction. It was the smirk of a man who was about to accomplish something. No worry, no doubt, and it frightened Frank, exceedingly.

The next morning. Frank strode past the receptionist in Jim's office, through the little railing around her desk. Jim called to him from within his office and told him to enter. The receptionist intercom was faster than Frank's feet.

"Good morning, Jim", said Frank, as he entered, "I . . ." but Frank dropped any sort of senseless pleasantry when he saw Jim. Jim was sitting behind his desk, tilted back in his swivel chair, a pile of money on the desk. His hands were together, fingers interlaced against his chin.

"Here's my half of the money", said Jim as he watched Frank watch the money. "Where's yours?"

"Uh, . . . oh, right here", stammered Frank as he pulled a neat packet out of his pocket.

"Good", said Jim. "Now what we'll do is put the money in a safe deposit box, and each of us will have a key. This way, either of us can draw the money without any fuss". Jim gathered the money from his desk, took Frank's packet, and said as he preceded him out of the office, "thus starts the diabolical scheme towards realization".

A week had passed since the money was deposited in the bank, since the hellborn idea was pushed into motion, but no further mention of the affair was to pass Jim's lips. Business transpired as usual, and a business-pleasure trip to Montauk Point was supported by many of the members of the club which Jim was the president and Frank was a member. So whole heartedly did Jim devise and applaud the venture, that all of the club members decided to go, including Frank. Frank's wife was persuaded to stay over at Jim's house, with Jim's wife, so that they might have a bit of relaxation together since, over the years, they had become great friends. Jim and Frank were to drive out together since, they too, were great friends. The trip was to begin in one day, and so completely was Jim's engrossment in the trip, that the idea of the murder seemed to have slipped his mind. Frank was well satisfied to wait and wonder, since he had only to gain . . . if not the hundred thousand—which he sorely wanted—at least the witnessing of the foul deed which could, in another way, be just as profitable

Each night they drove home in funereal muteness, which was Frank's indication that the murder was still pervading Jim's thoughts. On the eighth day following the agreement, Jim said that his plan was complete, and that he was ready to put it into action at any moment. Jim's heart leapt with satisfaction, or at least the anticipation that the thought of liberation brings.

"Well?" exclaimed Frank, unable to contain his curiosity.

"Well, what?" asked Jim.

"Tell me of your plan, . . . I mean, just how do you intend to kill your victim? First things first, who is going to be your victim and . . ."

"All in due time, Frank. You shall find out all about it in due time. Actually", Jim said as he leaned closer to Frank to enhance the secretiveness of the moment, and to insure privacy, "I'll tell you all about it tonight, before we leave for the Point. I think this evening is the time for it, just before we go away. We can say we were on the road to Montauk I'll have you for a witness, and they won't be able to even suspect me".

Frank's eyes widened with pleasure. "Yeah, you're right. I can tell whoever, we were together all the time. Tonight, hanh? Do you know your victim", continued Frank's curiosity.

"This evening, Frank", said Jim emphatically. "Now let me get some work done. I'll see you after work and tell you all about it".

Frank got up and headed for the door.

"Oh, Frank, wait a minute".

Frank turned quickly, thinking that Jim had decided to tell him now.

"Listen", said Jim. "I have a little gimmick ordered at a shop on Broad Street. It's one of those catchy little gimmicks that are a lot of laughs, and I have to pick it up before we leave. But, with planning and other things, I haven't got time to go and get it. I was hoping that you could pick it up for me. The shop closes at four-thirty".

"Oh, sure. I'll get it. Where's the shop?" said Frank.

"The address is 26 Broad Street, on the second floor. The name of the place is Quality Novelties, . . . but listen, no one is to know about this, so don't tell any of the boys, or anyone, for that matter, so when we get out there, it'll be a surprise, okay?"

"Sure, sure. I'll pick it up myself, later. When will I meet you?" asked Frank.

"I'll pick you up right in front of the place about four forty-five", said Jim.

"What about, ah, you know, the . . ."

"That comes between now and the time we head for the Point", said Jim. "Don't worry, I'll tell you all about it later".

"Okay, see you later", said Frank as he left Jim's office.

Jim watched Frank go out and of a sort of smirk wrinkled the corner of his mouth. Frank, for his part, was bewildered by the magnanimity of the situation, . . . murder. And Jim's uncaring, yea, even unfeeling attitude made him feel even more uneasy. He knew Jim though, and Jim never made wild boasts. He always hit his mark, . . . gad, what an appropriate metaphor, thought Frank as he entered his own office. *No doubt about Jim though*, thought Frank . . . *a perfect murder. It certainly will be perfect in more ways than one.*

At exactly 4:40, Jim got up from his chair, took his coat out of the closet, folded it over his arm, took his hat off the shelf, and stepped out of the door of his office into the outer office. He walked over to his secretary's desk, placed his hat down and said as he was slipping on his coat . . . "I'm going to leave now, Joan. Frank Graton was supposed to meet me here, but as usual, he's not here yet. I called his office and he's gone. I guess he's waiting by the car. Anyway, if anything comes up that you can't handle yourself, just ask Charlie Moreland, next door. He said he'd give you a hand if you needed him. I should be back in a few days, a week at the most".

"Yes, Sir. I'm sure I'll be able to handle everything satisfactorily".

"Good, well, so long", said Jim as he picked up his hat and headed to the door.

"Have a good trip, Mr. Ackland", called his secretary·

Jim's head twisted slightly sideways, and with a concealed smirk and a glance at the secretary from the side of his eye, said: "Thank you, Joan. I hope this to be a very profitable venture". The door shut quietly behind him. He pressed the little arrow shaped button that summoned the elevator.

Jim sat in his car, right on schedule, waiting for Frank to show up. As a matter of course, Jim, who was punctuality personified, expected to have to wait for Frank whenever they were to meet. He always had . . . even in college. Like the time someone was . . . someone was twisting the handle of the car door on the passenger's side back and forth, being restricted by the lock. Jim saw the familiar blue herringbone of Frank's overcoat and leaned over and pulled up the lock peg.

"Jesus, it's cold as anything out there", said Frank as he climbed into the car shrugging his shoulders closer together to create some body heat. "I was just calling your office. You must have given me the wrong address. There's no Quality Novelties in this building".

"No? I looked the address up in the telephone book", said Jim, thoroughly disconcerted. He glanced at his watch. "Too late now to even pick it up. Damn it all. Damn", said Jim disgustedly as he started the car.

Frank was blowing on his hands, rubbing them together as he turned to Jim. "Well, come on, what are you keeping all the wraps on this idea of yours for? Tell me about it will you, the suspense is killing me".

Jim nodded slightly with a chuckle. "Really", he said. "Let me give you my basic concept on the matter before I begin". He turned the car slowly into South Street toward the bridge. "Firstly, the main element of the murder must be surprise. That is, to take the victim while he is unaware of his circumstances. In this way he cannot retaliate nor even suspect . . . and therefore could not have told anyone of his would-be killer, or of his suspicions".

"You mean you should pick on a stranger that doesn't know you from a hole in the wall, and just sort of ambush him on a quiet street, and no one could possibly be the wiser", asked Frank, genuinely interested in figuring out the details.

"Well", said Jim, somewhat annoyed, "that certainly is a possibility, but I more or less considered that a lot less exciting than the plan I am about to unfold to you. True enough, you could do it very easily that way, but then, that's just the point. An ambush like that takes such little skill and real thought that the satisfaction derived from the challenge would be nil".

"Well, then, what? Do you think killing your wife, or your best friend, or someone close at hand to be a lot more exciting?"

"Exactly", said Jim.

"You must be kidding. You'd be implicated from the very outset. How far do you think you could get before they would arrest you", said Frank, thoroughly engrossed in the mysterious depths of the crime.

"Thou hast said it, Frank. The challenge is almost insurmountable . . . but the satisfaction derived from that type of crime, executed successfully, is tremendous. So you see, I've really given you the better end of this bargain by setting my sights so high", he laughed, "that's quite the appropriate expression, eh?"

"Yes", said Frank, quickly acquiescing. "Be more explicit. Just what is the rest of your plan?"

"Surprise, the first element, right?"

"Right", said Frank.

"The second is thrown in for spice, that is, someone who knows you, and he, in turn, is known to be a friend, or at least an acquaintance".

"You say him, is it to be a man?" asked Frank.

"Certainly. Not that there's anything wrong with women, but I've never even considered a woman for the victim. That's odd . . . now that you mention it . . ."

"Okay, okay, it's a man. Now what?"

"You're certainly in a hurry for me to commit this murder, aren't you?"

"I'm just curious to find out what's happening next, that's all".

"Third is nonchalance. You have to adopt an air of complete indifference, not to the crime of course, but to the investigation of your alibi, etc. I even think that if one went about trying to help solve the crime, his suspicion would be completely forgotten. Know what I mean?"

"No, not really", answered Frank.

"Well, the greatest asset that any criminal can have is casualness. Have you ever been doing something, and someone asked you what you were doing, almost inferring that you were doing something wrong, and you casually answered, why, I'm wiping the dirt off my shoes, or, I'm just replacing this pen, it fell on the floor."

"Well, sure, as a matter of fact, I have", answered Frank.

"Well, now, if you were really picking up a pen that you stole, or whatever, you wouldn't have been able to answer with such conviction, and then you would arouse suspicion. Now, if someone really were doing something wrong. but answered as calmly as if he weren't, well, people wouldn't suspect as quickly".

"But, they'd get on to you afterwards. That act can't hold up to facts", said Frank, trying to find holes in Jim's argument.

"Quite so, but the act is just for the beginning. As time passes, it is only facts and not apprehension that can convict you. Since in this instance there will be no facts, no clues, since I am going to completely get rid of evidence, and since I am not only not going to hinder the investigation, which is an act which would mark me guilty, but I intend to actually try and help find the evil-doer. I don't see how I could ever come under suspicion".

"How do you propose to get rid of the evidence", asked Frank.

"That's simple enough. There's lye, acid, deep forests, untrespassed places, and then or course, there's the river. A well-weighted body might never come to the surface".

Frank looked out of the car window on his side to the river that showed between long flat slips, and warehouses that resembled the heads of mute giants with their chins resting on the street level, looking out of square window-like eyes.

"If no one saw the weights, the body disappears, you act calmly, help with the investigation, have an alibi that will stand up . . ."

"Okay, what about the alibi?", asked Frank.

"That's the only real problem, but that too is simple and obvious. People have a tendency to make life, and in this case, death, more difficult than it really is. Take Poe's 'Purloined Letter'—ever read that story".

"Yes, that's where he leaves a letter right in the middle of the room and the police search everywhere, even under the wall paper, but never looked in the obvious places".

"That's right. Now if there is no evidence to work with, one can't be convicted in the first place, unless he is brought to suspicion by his absence. After all, the police realize you can get rid of a body. But now, if you were right in the midst of many people, or even a few of the right people, say the victim's wife, since we've established he's to be male, at the time of the perpetration of the crime, or the suspected time of the crime, well, they could never accuse you, could they?" said Jim.

"But how do you get to the wife at the right time, and kill the person at the same time?" asked Frank, somewhat perplexed.

"No one will know the exact time. It will only be calculated in hours of absence, and you could be far away before anything is known. Better still, if you were to bring the absence of the victim to everyone's attention, and began, together with the wife to look for the victim, well . . ."

"You've really got this all figured out, haven't you", said Frank as he looked from the window and the river to Jim, and then turned forward, somewhat nervous because of the hideous atmosphere in which he was riding. The bridge was just overhead. They were passing under it, as they did every night, left turn and onto the . . .

"Say, why are you turning this way? The bridge is the other way", said Frank in a quick, faltering way. "Why are you driving out to the wharfs?"

"Nothing. I'll just be a second", said Jim, calmly surprised at Frank's nervousness, then he turned to Frank, adding, "I'm just going to collect a bet".

THE LABYRINTH OF HAPPINESS

Rain billowed from the heavens. Outlined in front of the streetlight as I looked from my apartment window, the rain resembled thin cords of pulsating silver foil floating from the sky, winding and twisting in the wind. Spray bounced from the musty street, which was slowly losing its flat, lusterless charcoaled look. Little slick spots contrasted against the street here and there—now in greater profusion—and soon entire areas were completely covered with a slick blackness of wet reflecting a solid wedge of light from the drooping street lamp. From the level of the street arose the warm, all enveloping breath of dank, wet, dusty air which fills the first minutes of a rainy summer night with a strange, disagreeably nice, and so nostalgic an odor of past summers. I pushed away from the window frame and started toward the bathroom, my eyes still stiff with sleep. The outer edges of my eyelids felt inflamed and recoiled at the opening. I slid my hand against the smooth tiled wall and tripped the light switch. An image squinted at me from the silvery window on the wall.

"You must be crazy to be getting up at this hour", complained the image. "I must be crazy? Bob must be crazy! Out of his God damn clear head to call up at this hour and ask me to meet him. What the hell time is it?", I asked myself in the mirror, as I leaned forward and twisted the water faucet on the sink. "What the hell is the difference", I continued as I unbuttoned my pajama top, "I'm up now!"

The cold shock of the water on my face and neck sent a shudder through my body which subsided into full awakedness. I walked out of the bathroom into the bedroom and took my clothes from the silent valet.

"What the hell's the matter with Bob calling at this hour to meet him?" I began again as I slipped my trousers on and gave a sidelong glance at the clock on the night table. "One thirty?" It had seemed as if I had slept for hours. "Where the hell did he say to meet him, ... oh yeah, Pete's. Might as well get started". I finished tying my shoe laces, took a rain coat from the hall closet and bounded down the stairs. I opened the front door and was greeted by the hiss of bouncing rain. Little streams were running down next to the curb and under the wheels of the awaiting car, which resembled a soaking wet cat sitting patiently with little streams of running water sliding off its sleek side. I slid in and turned the engine over. She roared lustily. As I sat and waited for the engine to warm a little, I lit a cigarette. The wind shield wipers began making their familiar quarter circle of squeegeed glass, which was quickly redotted with water, and as quickly wiped away. I eased the car from the curb and headed toward Pete's.

The light from the inside diffused out through steamy windows that bore the owner's name in big old-fashioned gold letters. I pulled the car to the curb and went inside. Sitting at the bar, slouched on a stool, observing potent liquid mount the sides of his glass as he twisted it in his hand, was my awakener.

"What the hell is up, man?" I asked taking off my dripping rain-coat, hanging it on the little fingers of wood that stuck out from the wall. "Was it really this urgent?"

"Jesus, am I glad to see you, Don", said Bob with a look of wild, half bleary relief on his face. "When you hear what I tell you, you'll be staggered", he said with emotion, his eyes boring into me fiercely. "It sure staggered me!! I never believed it possible". His head nodded absently as his voice trailed off into silent, unbelieving contemplation. 120

"What is it?" I asked, concerned. "It better be pretty damn stagger-ing after getting me out of bed like this. Why the hell didn't you tell me yesterday afternoon when I met you at the plane?"

"I didn't know until tonight", he said as he grabbed my arm, "until I saw Gloria". The hurt that it became clear he was feeling, was transmit-ted through my arm. He pressed it in desperation.

"Ohh? What happened?"

His hand moved from my arm to the bar. He rested his chin upon a clenched fist. "I guess you know why the hell I went to California, don't you?" he asked.

I nodded I had, as I motioned the bartender to draw a beer for me.

"I went away so I could get enough money for Gloria and me to get married. I went away so we could get married", he repeated to himself in a voice hinting amazement, . . . "and I come back feeling bad enough about not having enough money, . . . well not having enough to, . . . as much as I wanted anyway, you know? I felt kind of down about that, but I thought that coming home'd have its compensations. I'd see Glo-ria and she'd understand, you know? And she'd help me to start over again. At least I figured she'd be something real that I could hold onto without it slipping away . . . I saw her tonight", he said flatly, almost with disgust. "You know, I told you I had a date with her?" I nodded. "Well we went for a long drive, and then for a drink somewhere in Westchester. She wasn't, . . . ohh, I don't know, she just wasn't with it, you know. She seemed to be thinking, or bothered about something. She was really, . . . uhh, moody. I asked her, what's the matter, and she said, 'nothing'. You know the way women have of saying nothing is bothering them and you know damn well something really is. I don't know if you're supposed to beg them to tell you or what, . . . but any-way, she kept saying that nothing was bothering her. Say bartender, . . . bring me another drink please. You want another drink, Don?"

"No, no thanks, I still have this beer in front of me", I replied.

"Thanks a lot, Joe", Bob said as the bartender put down his drink. "So she keeps this up for a while", he continued turning toward me, "and then she turns to me and says she thinks we should have a long talk and now was as good a time as any. I didn't know what to expect. I mean after going away to California and coming back feeling lousy, and now something is bothering my girl", he droned on in his half desperate, half pleading voice.

"She wanted to have a long talk with you, . . . what about?" I asked, urging him to continue.

"She told me, . . ." He stopped, turning to face me with narrowed, searching eyes . . . "Don, I asked you to come because I had to talk to someone, . . . I had to tell somebody, . . . and I wanted you to come because you've been my buddy for years. I want you to listen to this, and just tell me what you think".

"I'll try to help, Bob. What happened?"

"She said she wasn't sure anymore", he said with a horrendous finality mixed with embarrassment, "that she doesn't know if she loves me". He looked at me furtively for a moment to see my reaction then looked down. He was quiet now, taking a sip of his beer, lighting a cigarette. "While I was away she had to go out", he continued. "I told her to. You know, I didn't want her to stay home all the time, or to feel bad if she did go. I told her to go out and have fun, and not to feel bad about it. You know, just to have something to do. You just can't sit around all the time for four months", he said trying to explain.

"I understand. I don't think either of you could really expect the other not to go out while you were apart, and not be selfish", I said, trying to show I understood.

"Well, she started to pal around with the crowd that she used to before we met . . ."

"Which crowd is that, . . . the one in the Village?"

"No, . . . just the gang in her neighborhood. There's a whole bunch of people around there, and they throw parties all the time, and live it up. Anyway, she starts to go out with this crowd again, and in particular, she sees this guy Jim Sammison. She went out with him before she went with me. Well, you know how it is when you go around with a crowd, a lot of laughs, plenty of places to go, . . . you know, never a dull moment, lots of kicks. So, she starts to have fun running around the town again, like she used to. Not that she cared for this guy. She told me he doesn't mean anything to her, but they went out on a couple of dates. She just went out with him because I wasn't in town . . ."

"Okay. She's going out with the gang, and she went out on a couple of dates, . . . so? What about not being sure anymore? Where does that come in?" I asked.

"Well, going out with the gang I guess she got to think that maybe she didn't love me. Maybe, now that she was enjoying going out with others so much, she didn't want to settle down. Anyway, when I get home tonight she was bothered because she didn't know what to do. She doesn't care about this guy, it's that she's just not sure anymore about me". He stamped out a cigarette in the ash tray on the bar. "God! When she told me that, I almost went berserk. I was dumbfounded at first, you know, . . . then I saw red". His hands gripped the edge of the bar. "I got so angry I almost wrecked the place where we were. I just couldn't control myself".

"Take it easy, man", I said, trying to calm a new re-excited Bob, "you're getting all steamed up again".

"Yeah, I guess I do lose my head about it, . . . but why not, . . . I just can't understand it! Here I go away to build up enough money to get married, and she does this to me! That's what really hurts, . . . to think that she would do this", he said pounding his fist on the bar, his teeth gritted.

"Now wait a minute, . . . be reasonable. What did she do? She's lonely and she has some fun and she gets a little unsure of her love. You were gone for months, you weren't around, and she began to enjoy going with the crowd again. Now you're back and she is really confused, what's wrong with that? Would you rather she lied to you?"

"No, but . . ."

"No, but you don't want to hear the truth either. You don't really care about her, it's just the idea that she could throw you, the great Bob, over. If you were in her shoes and felt the way she does you'd probably tell her to go to hell and then you'd be sorry. So she's mixed up, . . . at least she's big about it. Give her some time, everything will straighten out".

"But what she did to me . . ."

"You don't own her you know! When someone loves you, it's supposed to be wonderful. She doesn't owe you anything. She doesn't have to love you. If she does it's great. If she doesn't, that's, . . . well, I don't know. Just give her time, she probably still loves you, . . . just a little mixed up".

"That's what she said, . . . give her a little time to figure it out. But I can't, not after what she's done".

"Oh, shit, . . . she hasn't done a God damn thing. Jesus, sometimes you're really thick headed. You're only going to ruin something that both of you wanted. She got a little doubtful, . . . but now you're back to reassure her and everything will turn out all right—if you don't mess it up with your big mouth".

"You really think so, . . . I mean really, . . . you're not just giving me a line of shit to calm me down".

"That's a nice thing to say. I get out of bed to meet you in the middle of the night, and you tell me it's a line of shit . . ."

"I'm sorry, I didn't mean that. I don't know what I'm saying. You really think it'll work out though, hanh?"

"Sure. She'll see that going out with the gang is kicks, but after all is said and done it means nothing. Love and all that is worth more than a few laughs. Just give her a little time", I said belaboringly, hoping to have made Bob a bit calmer.

"I told her I never wanted to see her again", he said angrily, now reliving the scene with her. "I told her that if she could do that to me I didn't want to have anything to do with her".

"Don't be so God damned silly. It won't kill you to give it a little time. What the hell is the difference? Besides, you'll be just as hurt if you don't . . ."

"What d'ya mean?"

"That if she leaves you, you'll be hurt whether or not you try to win her back, so you might as well try. At least you have a chance then. After she comes around a little bit your love will be twice as strong. Women are funny sometimes that way. They say things they don't mean. Just let it ride kind of easy, that's all. Forget about it, go out and have a good time, she'll fall in love with you and forget about the gang quick. Besides, if she doesn't come around its better to happen now than if you were married . . . no?"

"I guess, but, . . . ahh shit, man. It really knocked me out when she told me . . ."

"Of course it did, but what the hell are you, a love dictator? I can't see you letting your ego stand between the two of you. I'm not saying it's all your fault or anything. You're right, and I can see how you'd get very angry, . . . but what the hell. Her only sin was of unsureness. Give her a chance. If you really love her you will".

"But after what she did".

"Forget it. She didn't do anything that doesn't happen every day. Why don't you go home and sleep on the idea of just giving it a chance?" Joe the bartender moved down toward us. "Give me the check for both of us", I said. "I've got to get home", I said, turning to Bob. "I have to get up early".

"Okay. I'll take the check. I'm staying for another drink anyway".

"I'll stay and have one with you".

"No, I'd rather be alone. It's okay. Just let me be by myself for a while. I'll be all right. I'll call you in the morning".

"You sure?"

"Yeah, yeah, go on, go ahead back to bed", he said trying to smile, "and thanks a lot".

"Forget it. I couldn't let you down. Try to think about what I said and about the whole thing a little more calmly".

"Yeah, I'll try", he said as he twisted to Joe the bartender and ordered another drink.

"Good night", I called back as I pulled open the door and was greeted by a misty wind.

"Good night", said Bob.

"Good night now", said the bartender.

The air in Julius's was filled with that faint scent of stale beer, perfume, summer heat, sawdust and people that always seems to hang from the walls of a bar, just like the dust encrusted derbies that hang from Julius's wall and watch, and have been hanging and have watched generations go by. Those derbies have witnessed many a glance furtively thrown from one table to another; have watched many a couple walk out to some quiet rendezvous; have been there long enough to have seen the time when this here and now old woman sitting at a corner-table with grey straggly hair, a lined face bereft of ambition, of color, or beauty, the calloused hands, stood young and proud in the midst of the jubilant crowd, with her now tired head thrown high, her now retreating breast flaunting itself in front of the mustachioed young artist. The Derbies can remember how they left that evening, gay and happy, joking, perhaps just a little too full of drink, with shining eyes, flared nostrils . . . the Derbies witness now an old woman, shunned by other jubilant young, waiting, for whom, for what.

Suddenly, as if from a long forgotten dream, a face flashed before me, only to disappear past me. I twisted curiously to see this face that came from my long forgotten dream. Who is that face? Who? Gloria. Of course, Gloria, I said to myself as I remembered now. She looks at and past me, our eyes meet and there is something long forgotten, unconsciously rekindled. How many times, when she had been with Bob, had I looked into those same eyes, with the same expression in them, and now, how strange to look into them and have them turn away from me in unknowingness, as if I were encased in a wall, peering out from a hole, seeing, but being unseen. Her eyes return to mine. Now narrowing as they peer intently into mine, as if to discover the secret that we two share but can't remember.

"Don", she exclaimed, surprising herself with the recollection. "It's Don Wingate, isn't that it?", she said smiling as she approached my table.

"Yes, Gloria, that's it. How've you been?", I said, half rising.

"Oh fine, just fine, and you?", she said with a pleasantly surprised smile playing on her face. "Oh, I haven't seen you in, must be about two years. What've you been doing? Still at Bradbury's?"

"Yes", I replied, "still at Bradbury's. How did you remember that I worked at Bradbury's?" I asked curiously. "It's been such a long time".

"I've kept check on you, so you better be careful from now on", she said jokingly.

"No, seriously, it's surprising that you remember where I work after all this time. I can't remember where you worked".

"Oh, I've changed jobs since then. I'm with an advertising agency uptown now, Mill, Tonne & Shely. Ever hear of them?"

"No, I can't say that I have. Please sit down, . . . have a drink", I said, rising to offer her a chair.

"Well, only one", she said as I pushed her chair a little closer to the table. "I'm supposed to be with that short fellow over at the bar. The one with the glasses".

"He won't mind us having one drink, for old times' sake, will he?". I looked to the bar and saw a short fellow facing us from the bar, talking to another fellow.

"No, and even if he does, what the hell. I'd like a Tom Collins".

"Ray", I called to the waiter. "A Tom Collins. Gee, it's nice to see you again", I said to Gloria. "I've thought about you many times, you, and Bob, and . . . hope you don't mind my mentioning Bob".

"No, I don't mind. It used to hurt at first when anyone mentioned him, but now . . ." She shrugged, letting her voice trail off as she let a match book slip through her hand, and then reflected upon it as it lay on the table. She looked up at me inquisitively, her head tilted a little to one side. "Does he still work with you at Bradbury's?"

"No, he left about five months ago", I replied. "He works for some foreign import company downtown now. I talk to him all the time though, you know, still buddy buddy. That's why I think of you, . . . we used to have a lot of kicks when we went out on double dates and all".

"Yes, I know", she said somewhat sadly. Her eyes were alight with a melancholy glow. You could see Bob's face in front of her.

"Here's your drink", I said as the waiter placed a frosty glass in front of her. "I'm sorry if I make any sad memories come back".

"They're not sad, Don. It's sad that they are only memories though. Is he still, well, is he still the same Bob?"

"Yes, the same Bob".

"Is he engaged or married or anything?", she asked, trying not to show her inquisitiveness.

"No. He's going out with a couple of girls. Doesn't want to be tied down anymore he says. How about yourself. Engaged?"

"No, I haven't found anyone who was worth getting engaged to— except you, of course", she said trying to joke.

"I'm already spoken for. I don't think Bea'd appreciate my getting engaged to you too".

"Are you and Bea engaged?" she asked surprised.

"For a couple of months now. Don't know when we'll get married, but maybe soon".

"That's terrific", she said, smiling pleased. "Give Bea my regards when you see her, won't you?". She sat reflecting on things past.

"Sure", I said to break her melancholic mood. "It's too bad we can't all get together again for a date some one of these days".

"That would be nice, but you know how Bob is. He'd probably get angry if you even asked him. He was angry as hell the last time we went out wasn't he? Remember that night?", she asked shaking her head slowly and sadly. "It was a week after the big night when I told him . . . I don't even remember what I told him anymore, but he sure blew up. When we went out on that last date, the four of us, he just sat and brooded. Every once in a while he'd calm down and be himself for a couple of minutes and everything was so wonderful . . ." Gloria now reflected afar off, away from the conversation. Perhaps she again saw herself in Bob's arms, dancing. She stopped, then took a long draught from her drink, and looked across the table at me with a pathetic, half-hearted smile playing across her lips. "He ended that night when we went home telling me it would never work out. He said it would be better if I kept going out with the gang, having fun, and didn't worry about him. He was such a thick head. That was the last time I spoke with him. It seems like a nightmare I had a million years ago". She stared at the matches on the table.

"It does seem a long time", I reflected. "Oh, oh, here comes the little guy you're supposed to be with", I said as I caught sight of the short collegiate looking chap with heavy-framed glasses, walking toward our table.

"Say Gloria", he said inquiringly, "I don't mean to butt in, but did you even think that I might be worrying about you? Ted, Ted Knowles is the name", he said looking to me and extending his hand.

"Hi, Don Wingate, old friend of the family", I said as I gripped his hand. "Sorry to have held Gloria up so long. We were just reminiscing. Sit down, won't you?"

"Thanks. I've heard about you", he said, pulling a chair out and sitting down. "Gloria has mentioned you and the rest of the gang she used to pal around with quite a lot. All she talks about is the good times she had at this place or that place, with you and . . . oh what the hell is his name?" he said snapping his fingers as he lowered his head and brought his hand to his temple in a contemplative position. "Oh yes, Bob, Bob Keating, wasn't that it, Gloria?"

I looked at Gloria, who looked at me, a trifle flustered at the mention of her past life from the lips of a new friend.

"Yes, that's right, Ted, Bob Keating". She rested back into her chair and just stared across the table at me, not that she saw me. It was Bob that she saw through me, in me, because of me. We all sat and talked for a while, and had another round of drinks.

"Well Gloria, let's go", said Ted getting up, "we've got that party to go to. Nice meeting you, Don, perhaps we'll see each other again".

"Perhaps", I said as I raised myself partially out of the seat to shake his hand. Gloria got up, and Ted helped her with her jacket.

"Nice seeing you again, Don. Give everyone my love, won't you?", she said as she buttoned the jacket. She turned and they went out. Ted took her arm and they disappeared through the door, under the watching derbies.

"Sure, sure I will", I said half to myself as I sat down again and reflected on the now closed door. "Bob'll sure as hell be surprised to hear I met Gloria", thought I to myself. I shrugged and called the waiter.

The static in the earpiece was pulsated by the blaring of a buzzer. Finally there was a click in the mechanism and the other phone was lifted.

"Hello Bob", I said.

"Hi, Don, how's the boy", said the familiar voice.

"Ok, how're you doing?"

"Not bad. The usual kicks now and then. Where are you?"

"Downtown. I just came out of one of my favorite haunts. What are you doing?"

"Just sitting around recuperating from the week-end. Don, I'm telling you, . . . kicks! This was by far the greatest, and I really mean the greatest, week-end in the last year", he said with enthusiasm. He had really been living it up since Gloria.

"Sounds wild. Where were you?"

"We were at the Colas Hotel. You know that place that I go to every summer. Well, they had a reunion up there this week-end. It was wild".

"Really good, hanh?"

"The end. I don't think I got four hours sleep the whole week-end. Everybody was drunk as a skunk. I met a couple of nice girls while I was there. You should have seen this bit. All the guys and the girls are having this party, and every once in a while one of the guys would cut out with one of the girls, . . . and after a while they'd come back and then some other guy would cut out with the same chick, . . . or the guy'd cut out with another chick".

"Sounds like a lot of fun. You find anyone interesting during one of your exits out the side door", I asked. He laughed.

"Well there was this one chick, not a bad looking kid either . . . she was with some goose all night. He went for some drinks or something and she and I started to dance. Then we sort of disappeared out the side door. We walked down to my car. Boy, you should have seen that place. Every car in the lot was filled. A leg sticking out here, an arm there. All the cars were filled with couples. We got in the car and stayed there for a couple of hours, and later I drove to this all-night diner. Everybody and his brother from the hotel was there. It looked like everybody got up for breakfast, but it was four thirty in the morning. She was a pretty nice girl, . . . from Manhattan, in the eighties. I got her phone number. I'll have to try her some time. Promises to be an interesting night".

"You really meet a lot of chicks, don't you?" I said.

"Got to keep moving, don't you man? I met another one when I got back to my room. She was sleeping in my bed. I don't know how the hell she got there. So I just pushed her to one side and went to sleep. When we got up we had a nice long talk. I think I'll call her one of these days too. What's happening with you?"

"Nothing much. I was going to suggest that I come over to your place for a drink", I said.

"Sure, come on over".

"Okay, see you in about fifteen minutes". I hung up the telephone and got on the bus and started for Bob's place. He sure as hell is having himself a ball with all these girls he goes out with, I thought to myself. The bus moved down Third Avenue, past short-sleeve shirted men and cotton skirted women, who seemed to be acting out parts in a pantomime as the bus quickly passed them, making its way to the next stop.

"Funny guy, Bob. Out with all these chicks, having a ball". The bus' air brakes pulled the wheels to a halt. A man got in and the bus started up again . . . "Going out with all kinds of girls, and yet . . ." I remembered a girl that Bob had been friendly with. She was going out with one of the guys at the hotel. He told me she got plastered drunk, and her boyfriend, already sick from too much liquid refreshment, had passed out somewhere. There she was, loaded, knocking on Bob's door. He said, "I could've had anything I wanted. She even offered it to me, but you know, I just couldn't take advantage of her like that". So Bob took her in his arms and dropped her on the bed in his room and then went out again. She awoke the next morning and didn't even remember how she got to his room. "Nice guy, Bob, . . . got some principles". I reached up and grabbed the green cord that hung along the side of the bus. A little bell sound was heard. The bus pulled over to the side and the doors opened.

"Hey, Don", I heard my name being called aloud from above. I looked up and saw Bob at the window of his apartment. "Bring some ginger ale up with you", he called down. "You can get some in that store across the street".

I looked around. There was a delicatessen lit up with neon signs across the street. "Okay, I'll be right up". I went across the street and got two bottles of ginger ale.

"What do you want to drink?", Bob asked me.

"Give me some gin, straight".

"Here you go. So what's new, anything?"

"Not much. Still going out with Bea. How's Lillian?"

Bob shrugged his shoulders and sat down. "I don't know, Don. I think I'm going to cool it with this girl. I think I'm getting a little too involved".

It seems I've heard this statement ten times before. He'd say it toward the end of a time when he'd have been seeing Lillian regularly. And then every time he'd come back from the week-end where he met a lot of girls but none that really interested him, he'd say how much fun Lillian was and that this was probably the girl he was going to marry. "I don't know, you know? I think this week-end is going to be it", he said. "We're going away, and if I still feel this way I'm going to cool it"

I let the subject and the conversation drop. "I saw an old friend of yours tonight", I began again.

"Really? Who?"

"Gloria".

The name seemed not to phase him in the least, save that his eyes widened a little with curiosity. "No kidding", he said slowly. "How is she?"

"Fine. She asked for you. Said to give you her love". He was silently pleased by that.

"You know, we've often talked about her together, haven't we", he said reflectively, "and about how we should get together. I wonder if I should try her?"

"Well, I mentioned that we used to have a lot of laughs together, and why didn't we get together one night, just for old-times sake".

"What did she say?" he asked eagerly.

"She thought it was a good idea. Then we changed the subject".

"That might be interesting, you know, Lillian is going away for a few days, week after next. I might just ask you to call Gloria and, . . ." I made a face. "Well, I just couldn't call her myself", he began to explain. "Maybe you could call and say that it was your idea. Tell her perhaps you could arrange it with me if she were willing".

I shrugged. "Sure, I don't care".

"After all, she can only say no", said Bob. He looked at me in a slightly embarrassed way and then added "that's all it would be for, you know, for old times. She used to be a lot of fun, and like I said, she can only say no".

"That's right", I agreed. "I'll call for you if you want. Maybe the four of us could get together for a few laughs just like old times".

"Yeah, that would be kicks. As soon as Lillian goes away we'll make it".

The night went on uneventfully, except for sporadic mentions of Gloria and times past, and soon I took my leave of Bob. But it never left me for a minute, that is, the feeling that Bob, . . . well, it seemed to me that underneath the grease paint Pagliacci was crying, only he didn't know it. We resolved to get in touch with Gloria the following week, but as it happened we didn't. Lillian didn't go away, and then

Bob got into one of his stages when he was going to marry Lillian, so the reunion was put off indefinitely

I met Gloria again, more than ten months later. She was married by then. Married to the fellow I had met in the bar that night. I don't even remember his name now, Ted something or other. I do remember her though, same gleam in her eye, still asking about Bob. I wasn't sure why she asked, but it seemed that she still thought warmly of Bob.

The next time I saw Bob was at his apartment. I told him about the meeting. "I met Gloria a couple of days ago, Bob".

"No kidding?", he said slowed by amazement, with the same amount of interest he had shown on previous occasions.

"Yeah, she's married", I said hesitantly.

"Married?" he said in a dumbfounded way, with the utmost of surprise, as if some impossible thing had happened. "Who did she marry?"

"Some guy, name of Ted, . . . I can't remember his last name. I met him that last time I met her".

"Is he a nice guy?"

"Nice enough. I didn't get to know him very well".

"Gloria married, . . . I never thought of her as being married. You remember how she and I were supposed to get married. That seems like a hundred years ago". He was now far off, thinking, just staring over my head at the wall behind me.

"Yeah, it does seem like a long time ago", I said. "Nice girl, Gloria, really nice".

"You're right", he said, nodding his head in agreement. "I hope that guy is nice enough for her. She deserves a good break. She's had it rough enough. Maybe I should call her and wish, . . . no, I don't think I'd better. I hope she'll be happy. That's more than she would have been with me", he assured me, looking to see if I believed him.

"Yeah, guess so", I agreed. He lit a cigarette, and inhaled, looking at me, smiling wearily to reassure me.

"What do you want to drink?"

"Gin is good".

He handed me a glass, and sat in a chair across the room, and he now stared at me over the rim of his glass, his smoking cigarette in his hand. He didn't see me though, just sat there reflecting.

"I'm going to take off, Bob. I've got to meet Bea", I said after a long silence.

"Yeah, yeah sure. I've got to go out soon myself. One of the chicks from the hotel".

"One of your wild flings again?"

"Yeah, you should be single like me, man, a different chick every night if you want".

"I'll give you a call in a couple of days", I said backing to the door.

"Yeah, . . . take it easy".

"Take it any way you can get it", I said jokingly.

"Ain't that the truth", he said laughing a little, looking at me with those sad, frightening eyes. He closed the door, and I walked down the stairs and out into the street.

THE BALLAD OF THE
RUMBLING SUBWAY

Standing on tile tomb like platform, looking down the empty tunnel,
    I behold in the inky gloom, gleaming lines aparallel.
        Little green, red, and yellow lights glowing in the darkness,
            waving messages of warning to the rumbling express
as it travels through the umbrageous steel forest.

Suddenly, afar off, we espy
    the advancing; giantess, one green, one red eye.
        Two little twinklings flickering to and fro,
            as the writhing monster emits a screaming bellow . . .
piercingly goading a city at rest.

The air is thrummed by a pounding pandemonium . . .
    pulsating, throbbing, erupting, in my cranium.
        Whiffing within reach blurs a flickering glare . . .
            clic-clacking unending, then a pff't of air,
the brakes upon the wheels hard prest.

The doorman presses a button, the gate whirrs open;
   there's the transfer of humanity, the dropping of a token,
      a rapid shuffling of feet as the door slides closed . . .
         . . . stopped by an arm interposed.
Another victim the train is wont to digest.

Sitting on the tossing chair,
   one is immedeately brought to stare,
      at the fantastically strange surrounding,
         with mysterious and odd sights abounding . . .
like a tattered man asleep with his head upon his chest.

Off in a corner one can see
   an unabashed true love, girl upon his knee.
      The conductor must keep orderly his train
         and requests the couple to kindly refrain,
lest . . .

On their arrival at the next destination
   he will certainly summon the guard of the station.
      Who will, according to his disposition
         be forgiving or demand contrition,
and thereupon arrest.

The epileptic train seems to be slowing,
   the passengers to alight allowing.
      At the next stop which is twenty third
         there appears a person seemingly absurd,
dressed in the native habit of, perhaps, Budapest.

He adds his figure to the seated congregation,
   who all told represent almost every nation.
      Some of whom may have been kings and queens,
         soon to be pressed and pushed like sardines,
when our train, the rush hours infest.

But now the subway enjoys its daily sleep,
   as slowly through the tunnel the trains creep.
      In a few short hours to awake,
         to footsteps resounding like a quake;
jamming the train, till sides protest.

People, people, people, that's all that one can see,
   save for an advertisement for the tuna, 'Bumble Bee.'
      Women, men, girls, and boys and some hard to define,
         jam together, twine, incline, entwine, and intertwine,
and unknowing people, some erotica will molest.

Times Square, 59th street, Wall Street, Bowling Green
   have people delivered to them, in number umpteen.
      Masses arrive to perform their daily chore,
         to earn enough coin to keep the wolf from the door . . .
and a little extra that the banks will invest.

Change for the express at Pacific stop.
   The door slides open, people jump out to swap.
      Others cram in, push prod, jab, jolt,
         butt, beat, tap, thwack, and always it's the other's fault,
as the bruises on your shin attest.

Excuse me, excuse me, please,
   I implore, as through the mass I squeeze.
      Squirming, pulling, laboriously trying,
         An effort which gets me off . . . exhaustingly sighing,
with one of two buttons gone from my vest.

Kleins, Macy's, and Gimbels, not to mention Ohrbachs,
   have stock in trade overflowing their racks,
      while buyers are sped to the mecca of retail
         in a car impelled by an electrified rail.
Midday, these, our electric congest.

The end of the line finds the train tenantless.
   The conductor snares papers for the press,
      deserted by their buyers, full of news hum-drum,
         their sale gives the collector an extra income . . .
which is the reason he gathers with such zest.

Rush hour again, and again all the pulling,
   the labor involved is something grueling.
      Homeward bound the office workers speed,
         clic-clacking along on the mechanical steed,
which is the worse wear in the daily contest.

Peacefully now the train ambles along,
   quavering a most dissonant song,
      while in its belly snoringly sleep
         some of the students from Bowerie prep.
Heads hung on their chest.

I alight from the train weary and bewildered,
   and view the return trip with the utmost of dread.
      For tomorrow and tomorrow, and the day after that,
         today's battle will be repeated tit for tat,
as the train travels through the umbrageous steel forest.

Forward noble chariot of steel,
   forward let roll your wheel.
      Carry your passengers both big and small,
         to their home, their work, or their ball,
and woe be unto him who leaves you unblest.

Woe unto him who leaves you unblest,
as you travel through the umbrageous steel forest.

A WOMAN CRIES IN HER SLEEP

The night was quiet; the stillness, the late hour, the dormant wind created a vacuum effect. Now a sound. The powdery snow crunched beneath the feet of a lone figure hastening past the silent, snow-capped steps of the dark brownstones. The man's shadow skimmed out over the white surface of the sidewalk, getting smaller as he approached the street lamp, then expanding again as he strode past it into the darkness of the valley between the lamps. It was cold, that cold, that clear, crisp cold that exhilarates the body, that made one want to fill one's lungs with all of this clean air.

Carl breathed in fully of the fresh air about him and held his breath with his lungs filled to an overwhelmed capacity of cleanness. He exhaled, and a wisp of steam escaped from his mouth. Oddly enough, even in this wonderful environment of freshness, Carl still faintly detected Ruth's perfume. He had been so close to her, to that fragrance that seemed always to hover about her; he could smell it in her hair, on her skin, on her bedclothes, . . . perhaps it was his imagination conjuring the sensation of her fragrance. He sniffed the lapel of his coat to determine if the perfume accidently embedded itself there when he kissed her good-night. His lapel smelled like moist wool.

Funny, he thought, *I swear I still smell that perfume*. He continued his pace. *What a great night*, now remembering Ruth. The scent must be imagination. "I should have had the night attendant drive me home; damn garage is too far from the house", he murmured.

The wind, suddenly and without warning, arose from the ground violently, and swirled upward and around, carrying with it a bitter lashing cold that seemed to pass through Carl's body. He bundled the lapels of his overcoat together, and leaned into the wind. It began to flail him, his face, his ears, it beat against his eyelids until he had to close them, opening them only blinkingly to see if he were headed straight. Finally he reached his stoop and bounded up the stairs over the white mantle from the skies. A renegade wind swept down quickly from the roof of the house, hugging the building, viciously lashing out at and carrying with it, Carl's hat. He whipped his hand up to grab it; too late. It was torn from his head, and twisting through the air, thrown down on the sidewalk.

"Son of a bitch", he murmured, "just when you're freezing your ass off", he said to himself, annoyed, as he trudged down to the foot of the steps, picked up the hat, and hastened up the steps again, and through the door.

He walked quietly down the flight of steps leading into the sitting rom so as not to disturb Ginger. Ginger was Carl's wife. A most loving wife was she, as he was a loving husband. He walked lightly not so that she would not find out he was coming home late, but that she would not be disturbed. Ginger didn't mind him coming in late, or even that he might be out with other women. One thing about this marriage, he made sure it was understood, that each of them must have their own friends, their own diversion. They understood each other perfectly, . . . and they understood their marriage perfectly, and no stilted or stagnant ideas of propriety ran their lives . . . quite the opposite. They ran their own lives and decided for themselves just what was proper, and what was not.

Carl walked slowly and carefully, his eyes being unaccustomed to the dark—especially coming in from the snow outside. As he neared the candle that was left on the table in the living room as a night-light for him, he moved more easily. He gazed into the smoked mirrors on the wall behind the table, and with the complementary light from below flickering on his face, framed on the bottom by a loosened tie, and on top by imperceptibly disheveled hair, he thought how lucky women in general were that he existed. Most other men were not even a match for him. His looks stunned, his charm and tenderness overwhelmed. *Ah Ruth, you lovely, sensual woman, you . . . how lucky you have been tonight*, thought Carl to himself.

Looking up he noticed in the mirror the reflection of the mobile design, the Christmas one, with colored balls and holly dangling from its suspended wires, was twirling, vibrating, twisting around, just as it did when he passed it and disturbed the air that surrounded it when he passed it on his way to the office every morning. A quick shock of air filled the room as the front door banged against its frame.

Carl twirled. "Who's there?" he called into the darkness. No answer. Peering blindly, he repeated his question to the room that seemed to close in upon him. Again there was no answer. Cautiously, not knowing what awaited him, who or what was there in the dark, he slid his hand slowly over the wall toward where he knew the light switch to be. He felt the switch, flipped it with trepidation and anticipation. The normal pieces of squat low furniture, the vivid pastels, were all that greeted him. It had sounded like someone going through the doorway, but who would it have been. Ginger? He walked back to the bedroom and flicked on the light. Ginger's head lifted from her pillow. Squinting, she opened one eye, firmly holding the other closed against the glare of the light.

"I just heard the front door bang shut. I thought you went out", said Carl.

She smirked annoyance. "Yes, I did".

"That's funny". Carl turned back into the sitting room. He walked through the room, up the stairs, opened the front door, and looked outside. The street was empty and white. Turning to go in, he saw many footprints in the snow on the steps, many more than he would have made walking over the purely driven snow. *It must have been someone*, he thought. *I heard the door bang*, . . . and now the footsteps, the mobile moving, as if someone had passed by and gone out. A faint gleam of suspicion flickered into bloom within him.

"Ginger, baby", he called in a somewhat knowing way as he walked back to the bedroom, "are you sure you didn't hear anyone?"

"Course I'm sure. You were the only one I heard when you came in."

"You heard me come in, but didn't hear anything after that?" he asked doubtingly.

"No!" said Ginger, exasperated.

"That's strange. The door slammed, the mobile was moving, there were more than one set of footprints on the stoop and there weren't any before I got here", he said sarcastically. "Perhaps your lover was a little hasty in his departure, eh?", said Carl, jokingly serious. This flickering suspicion began to obsess his thoughts. He didn't mind her having friends and all that, but an affair, . . . and in his own bed. He slyly studied more closely Ginger and the bed, as he leisurely took off his jacket. The bed was completely disarranged and rumpled as if there had been much activity thereon. He now meticulously observed the room as he began to undress, feeling that he was shrewdly uncovering a poorly concealed affair.

"You'd better tell your friend to be more careful next time", said Carl. "You almost got caught", he said, affecting detached amusement.

"What in God's name are you talking about now? Can't you just shut up and let me get some sleep. I haven't been able to sleep all night".

"He must be pretty good, hanh?"

"Yes, he's very good", said Ginger sarcastically, trying to agree with Carl, to silence him, "so much better than you, in fact, that we were making love without a rest all night".

"Are you serious about this?' Carl said, suddenly outraged. "I mean, I don't like fooling around about this sort of thing . . ."

"Then shut up and stop being such a child. I haven't been able to sleep all night, and now you come home and start some nonsense about my lover being here . . . grow up. Do you think I'm crazy to have someone here?"

"I heard the door slam, . . . there are footsteps on the stoop—come out and see them yourself, and you tell me it's nonsense. You've got a hell of a nerve, you, you, goddamn tramp, bringing somebody here while I'm out".

"Why you nervy son of a bitch", screamed Ginger angrily. "You rotten, hypocritical bastard . . . to stand there and call me a tramp", her voice was reaching an emotional peak. Tears began to well up in her eyes. "You, big understanding man, so mature, such a great lover, . . . 'we must all have our own friends, dear' ", she said mimicking his words in a cutting, invective way, " 'you know, to sort of keep up with the styles. This way we'll always be interesting to each other' ".

"I told you we should have our own friends", Carl said defensively, "but I don't intend to have you in bed with all sorts of guys, . . . my own bed, . . . what the hell do you think I am a fool, . . . cuckolded in my own house?"

"Well, if you spent more time in your own house, maybe you wouldn't have so many stupid suspicions. Come home once in a while instead of taking some of your little chippie friends to bed. Where the hell were you tonight?"

"I was out with Tom Jordan and Billy Gregor . . ."

"You're a goddamn liar and you know it. Don't hand me that nonsense. You still smell of perfume, you dope", she said groundlessly.

Carl wasn't sure he smelled of perfume; he had thought he smelled the scent about himself. His consciousness of guilt and Ginger's unwitting but ever so deft thrust put Carl in a defensively uncomfortable situation.

"There are other women in the world you know. We were at the Club Lido and we met a couple of girls from Billy's office. They sat and had a drink with us, and that's about it. So don't try to shift the blame to me. You had somebody here, didn't you? Didn't you?" asked Carl, who seemed prone only to an affirmative answer. Trust between men and women is a very incomprehensible thing. A man feeling a woman has done wrong will not completely believe her if she says she didn't, . . . he will always have a lurking suspicion he has been lied to, . . . and if the woman says she has done him wrong, he'll believe her and be completely crushed. Trust is something that has to come from within. In order to trust another, we have to trust ourselves first.

"Look, you fool", said Ginger in an enforcedly calm, but nonetheless emotional way. "I was here all night, tossing and turning, trying to sleep . . ." She began to cry softly. "You were out running around, and you tell me that someone was here? You miserable bastard, you rotten, rotten", Ginger slumped on the bed, crying vehemently.

"Now, Ginger, . . . it's just that I came in and the door slammed, and the footprints, and the mobile, and all, . . . well, what's a guy supposed to think? I mean . . ."

"If you don't believe me, ask Mary", cried Ginger, lifting her head. "I called her up to come over and stay with me for a while because I couldn't sleep. Call her up and ask her who was here. Go on, call her . . . call her", sobbed Ginger as her head slumped down on the bed and she cried all the more in her pillow.

"Baby. . .", said Carl entreatingly as he crossed the room and sat on the bed next to Ginger. He stroked her hair. "It's just that . . . well, it's just that I'm so afraid someone will steal you away from me. I'm sorry I said what I did. I didn't mean it. I just jumped to a conclusion. I'm sorry baby. Please stop crying".

But Ginger's crying persisted. "You miserable bastard, you miserable bastard", she sobbed over and over. Carl began to feel shameful and terribly childish.

After about thirty minutes her crying subsided into a whimper and Carl lifted her into the bed, and slid in next to her. "I'm sorry, baby, please forgive me".

"It's all right, . . . forget it", Ginger said with that nasal quality that comes after lamentations.

Carl switched off the light, and put his head back on the pillow. From the living room came the faint flickering yellow glow of the candle that he forgot to extinguish when he came in. He folded back the covers, slid his feet into his slippers and scuffed into the living room. The wind that had begun to wail sent blasts against the window panes and door, banging them in place. Hanging above the candle, the mobile was still twirling as it had been when he came in. He couldn't comprehend the reason for the movement. It was dangling and turning as if someone had brushed into it. He looked around, but there was no one. Putting his hand up, he stopped the motion of the mobile, and when it was perfectly still, loosened his grip on it. Immediately it began to slowly twirl again. He put his hand up to stop it again and as he did, he felt the current of warm air rising from the flame of the candle. Now he realized that it was the heat waves, the expanding of the warmed air, that was moving the mobile. Slowly, he blew out the candle, the instigator, the fuse for his powder keg of guilty suspicion, and walked back toward the bedroom.

As Carl entered the room, he heard Ginger softly whimpering. She was crying again. Carl slipped into the bed and whispered, "I'm sorry baby". He slid his arm around her shoulder, but she twisted away. Perhaps, he thought it would be better to let her cry. It is so difficult to argue with the flowing tears of a woman. He turned up and stared at the greyish, purplish ceiling, . . . and as he dozed off, he could hear the continued sobbing of his wife as she lay next to him.

The warm water was running over his head, and Carl was thinking to himself how foolish he was to suspect Ginger. The thought of her being unfaithful disturbed him, to say the least, although it wasn't really the infidelity that bothered him, but the idea that his wife would need another man, and the fact that if found out, well, . . . it always hurts a libertine's pride to find out his wife is unfaithful. No, Ginger wouldn't fool around, she's too good for that sort of thing, he thought hopefully as he dried himself off. He dressed and walked into the bedroom. Ginger was awake, lying in bed, visibly showing signs of a sleepless, crying night.

"Darling, let's forget about last night. I'm sorry . . ."

"That's all right, Carl, I've forgotten it already".

"Thanks dear", he said as he kissed her forehead. "I'll try to give you a call from the office later. I don't think I'll be home till late tonight . . . have to meet one of the boys from the New Jersey office".

"That's all right. See you later".

"So long", said Carl as he mounted the stairs and went out the door. The slamming door sent a slight shock through the house, but Ginger was already too occupied dialing the phone to pay much attention to the percussion. She waited as the number she called rang.

"Hello Frank, Frank Darling", she said as tears began to well up in her eyes. "I've been so miserable without you". Tears flowed down her cheeks. "Please let's never fight like that again. I don't think I could stand being away from you for two days again".

She listened to the voice on the other end of the line. "Yes, . . . yes, I couldn't sleep all night, just thinking that I might never see you again". She hesitated, listening. "I love you too. I'll get dressed and come right over". She puckered her lips, sending an electronic kiss, then she hung up, and swung quickly out of the bed.

A NIGHT AT THE CARNAL-VILLE

Roger's large figure pushed up a long bulge in the bed covers that re-sembled a miniature mountain range, like the fake mountains that you can buy for the settings of electric trains. You would almost expect a little black locomotive, with its searching head beam, its frantic little wheels spinning, to come steaming out from behind his feet, one of which stuck out from beneath the covers into midair only to swerve and disappear in the dark cavernous tunnel that was dug in under the highest mountain near his hip. It was a dark shadowed spot where gen-tly sloping folds of covers cut off the light of the moon which passed through the window and between the parted curtains, with a shin-ing blue-grey luminance. Roger lay on his side, asleep, his thin-frame glasses still clenching the small of his nose, his arms folded over the evening papers, which were strewn over the floor as well as the bed.

Soft shadows fell fleetingly across his sleeping countenance, as the face of the moon became shadowed fleetingly by small silvery translucent clouds in silhouette, . . . emerging brighter than before—making all the world blue-bright and extremely quiet.

It was about 1 a.m., and in Tylersville everyone, or at least all the nice people were quite asleep. The ancient boards of the front porch, as someone walked slowly across them, pierced the crisp quiet of the house. Roger turned restlessly in his bed. He was a light sleeper at times, times, that is, when he sleepily waited for Nancy to come home. He could awaken at the slightest sign of her return, and after she was safe, after his thoughts were turned only to sleep, he slept with the determination of a tired bear at the dawn of winter.

The squeaking stopped, only to be replaced by the whine of the front door opening slowly. It closed quickly, and feet shuffled across the threshold into the living room which stood behind the sliding doors to the left of the staircase.

"Shhh", rasped Nancy, who was Roger's only child, a fair haired, attractive—when all dressed-up—girl of nineteen, "watch out for that chair . . . shh . . ." she rasped again as the fellow she was directing tripped into the chair she had warned him about. Nancy contained her laughter only by putting her hand over her mouth. She motioned her follower forward again, still containing her laughter with her hand.

Upstairs, Roger heard the slight whump of the chair as it slid against the floor. His eyes opened, but his body moved not. Now he could distinctly hear the living room doors slide open, then slide closed again. He slipped his feet down and into the slippers which were under his bed. He. kicked the newspaper out of the way and found the one slipper that was buried beneath it. As he took his robe off the chair by the window, he saw a light snap on from the living room, throwing a square of greenish white on the shadows about the house. It must be Nancy, he thought, but even so, it wouldn't hurt to check. Besides, he wanted to tell her to come up to bed soon. He didn't like her sitting in the living room with men until all hours of the night. It just wasn't proper. The way those college men from the school were these days, a good girl just isn't safe, anywhere, not even in her own home.

A long slit of light was the target to which Roger's eyes were drawn as he made his way stealthily down the stairs. Not that he was trying to be stealthy, but the dark and the night and the quiet invaded his descending figure. He did not know who it was down there, that was it, it could be a burglar. He wasn't trying to sneak up on his daughter and her date. He didn't know who it was. He reached the door. Beyond he heard the rustle of silk and crinoline and nylon. It was Nancy, after all. Silently, he slid the door open, and there, sitting on the couch was the couple, kissing. Nancy's date was embracing her, with his back twisted toward Roger.

"Hhhhrrmpph", sounded Roger, as he stood at the door. Nancy's date, a fellow that Roger had never seen before, twisted around quickly, as Nancy's hands smoothed her dress and her hair in one motion. They both sat surprised and somewhat shamefully looking at Roger. "Well, what's the idea of this?", said Roger, fiercely indignant. He stood confronting the pair, waiting . . . "Well, what the hell is going on here?" repeated Roger, his head bobbing to emphasize his words.

"Nothing at all sir", said the fellow rising slowly, hesitantly. "I was just, . . . well, I was . . ."

"I know damn well what you were doing boy, I know damn well", fumingly spumed Roger. "I was young once, too. But I never got carried away with myself. We respected women in those days. You've got a hell of a nerve to be coming into my house, and making love on my couch . . ." Roger was gesticulating and shaking his head for emphasis.

"Oh Dad, be serious", Nancy said, weepfully embarrassed.

"That's enough, Nancy, go to your room", Roger turned to her imperiously. "I want to speak to this young man alone . . ."

Roger turned back to the young man in front of him, who stood akimbo, biting his lip nervously, annoyedly shifting from one foot to the other. Nancy, as she left, shrugged her shoulders in signal to her date, as if to say, "I'm sorry, . . . it will only be a short ordeal".

"Listen here young man", began Roger after listening for Nancy's tread ascending the stairs. "I don't want this sort of carrying on going on in my house", he said slamming dust off the table as his hand came down heavily. "This is a respectable house, and a respectable little town, and I won't stand for this sort of thing. What are you little wise acres making of this town, . . . a cat house . . . you God damn college wise guys. What do you think my daughter is, . . . kisses every fellow that takes her out. I don't mind you kids going out and having a good time, but God damn on this sort of nonsense . . . don't let me see this sort of thing around here again, you hear me?" raged Roger with eyes that almost glared out of his head, pointing his finger in the fellow's face. Roger's austere, round face, with the glasses still grasping the nose, had flushed to a purplish red, even his bald pate was colored with the flood that he had summoned to give him strength for screaming. He towered above the seated young man.

"Yes, sir", said the young man, more to end the ordeal and get home, than in sincerity. "I'm sorry it had to happen . . . I'll be sure it never does again", he said, knowing that was what Roger wanted to hear. *Shit on you, you antiquated bastard*", the young man simultaneously thought to himself, *evil minded old bastard.*

"This is a nice town we have here, and we don't allow none of the fooling around they do in the city. Let's see it doesn't happen again", said Roger to the young man as he guided him to the front door and watched him go down the steps of the front porch.

Roger stood in his bathrobe, leaning against the column that supported the roof of the porch. The moon bathed the porch and Roger in blueness.

When the sound of the disappearing car had also disappeared, Roger turned into the shadows, shut the door, bolted it with the double bolt and went up the stairs. *Have to get some sleep*, thought he to himself. "Bill'll be over at eight thirty to drive me to the airport. Big day tomorrow" Roger was envisioning his trip to New York and the business meeting there tomorrow night.

"Nancy", Roger whispered as he gently knocked and then pushed open her door.

"Yes, Dad?" said Nancy in an exasperated way.

"I know it wasn't your fault, baby", he said as he sat at the edge of her bed, "but I want you to be more careful. These men these days, they don't care for a woman", Roger continued slowly, emphasizing each word. He cupped his hand behind Nancy's head, caressing the soft hair that fell to her shoulders. "You have to be careful all the time . . . it's not like when I was a boy. We respected women then".

As he stroked Nancy's hair, Roger felt a warm moisture transferred to his arm from her cheek. She was crying. "I'm not trying to tie you down, honey", he said assuringly, "I'm just doing these things for your own good. I wouldn't want anything to happen to you".

"I'll be very careful from now on", Nancy said resignedly.

"Good girl", said Roger as he kissed his daughter on the forehead. "And we won't say anything about this to mother, okay, honey?"

"Thanks, Dad", Nancy said as she was expected to do.

"Good night, dear".

"Good night, Dad".

"Listen, Rog, ol' boy", said Charlie, a heavy jowled, rotund faced home office representative, who was showing Roger New York, "I have just the place for us, a little spot downtown where they have a terrific show".

"Well, now, Charlie, I don't know. I have to get up early in the morning . . . I've got that plane to catch".

"Oh, c'mon, . . . just a little while. It's only eight thirty. Driver, take us down to Third Street and Sixth avenue", said Charlie to the cab driver.

"Well, okay, but let's not stay out too late. I've got that plane to catch. So, you really think that this deal with Morgan will go through, eh?" asked Roger.

"Sure, sure it will, but let's not talk business now. We're going to a joint where you'll see the curviest broads in town", said Charlie devoured by a carnal anticipation.

"Oh, one of those places, eh?", asked Roger awakening. "What is it, Charlie, one of the stripper joints?" concluded Roger with wide eyes.

"That's a nice name for it", Charlie snickered. "Over in this place they take off what the other places leave on . . ."

"Sounds like you know the right spots, Charlie", Roger smiled.

"Got to keep the boys from the field happy, eh Rog?", said Charlie, slapping Roger's arm for emphasis.

"Did you say the boys from the feel?", said Roger, bursting with laughter, pounding Charlie's arm.

"Yeah, the boys from the feel", repeated Charlie, laughing loudly, grasping Roger's arm as he swayed with amusement.

"Here you go, Mac", said the driver as he U-turned and stopped on the corner of 3rd and Sixth Avenue.

"Here are the places, Roger", said Charlie looking up as he ducked out the cab door. "Take your pick. The Blond Bombshell over there" . . . Charlie pointed to the different illuminated signs hanging from the joints along the street. "Candy Doll over there, and Sugar Baby over there. Which one do you want to hit first?"

"Let's see—that Blond Bombshell. I always did like blonds", said Roger, laughing. Both men were laughing as the eager doorman, a military peaked cap on his head, opened the door for them.

Inside there was only gloomy darkness, relieved by dim yellow lights. On one side behind the bar, the lights revealed shadowy people. A rectangle of blue lights outlining a stage was lit up against the far end of the club. Within the frame of the stage lights was a woman with stringy black hair, too old to strip anymore, who introduced herself as the Mistress of Ceremonies—quite the appropriate description— Standing at the bar, behind a velvet cord suspended between thick chrome poles that kept them herded together like cattle, were a number of men, in one state of excitement or another. At the entrance end of the bar, near the front of the club, were girls, who shifted on their stools as Roger and Charlie walked to the bar.

"Want to sit at a table or stand at the bar", asked Roger, twisting to Charlie who was behind him.

"Let's stand at the bar. This way we can duck out to one of the other joints if this one isn't hot, and I mean hot", said Charlie breaking into a leering laugh.

"Give me a scotch and soda", said Roger to the bartender who had come over to get their order. "What are you drinking Charlie?"

"Give me a, . . . well, make mine the same".

Hoarsely talking from the stage, the MC, who was in front of the closed stage curtain, said, . . . "and now we want to present to you, the one, the only wowww, . . . hey—take it easy back there boys", she said as she moved the lower part of her body away from the curtain, as if it had been grabbed suddenly from behind. "I don't mind the ring, but the wrist watch?"

"Ha, ha, . . . not the wrist watch", laughed Charlie gleefully. "What a crazy place, hanh, Roger?" he said turning to Roger so they might laugh together.

"Sure is Charlie", said Roger paying more attention to the small blond girl at the end of the bar, who was demurely smiling back as Roger looked her way.

" . . . yeah, I'm part Spanish and part Scotch", continued the MC, "hot and tight".

"Hot and tight", laughed Charlie as his elbow dug into Roger's arm . . . "you hear that, Rog, hot and tight?"

"Hey, Charlie, watch, you'll make me spill the drink", admonished Roger as he was clinking his glass against the one he had just bought for the little blond from the end of the bar, who was now sitting next to him. "Charlie", said Roger as he tapped on Charlie's shoulder, "Charlie, this is Marie".

"Say", said Charlie admiringly, "you're a pretty fast worker, aren't you Roger. I didn't know you still had it in you", Charlie said starting to laugh.

"You sometimes get the best tune from an old piano", said the blond.

Roger smiled. "See Charlie, . . . women know a good thing when they see it".

Charlie turned back to the bar and ordered another drink, then he turned to Marie. "Listen, Marie, why don't you invite one of your friends over here to have a drink with me. How about that red-head", said Charlie, glancing toward the end of the bar. "Hey, where'd the red-head go?"

"You mean Red Hot?" said Marie. "She's on now". Marie nodded toward the tall red-haired girl who was now walking toward the stage. She disappeared behind the curtain.

"She gonna dance now?" asked Charlie.

"Yeah", said the blond finishing her drink.

"Want another drink?", asked Roger.

"Well, if you insist", said the blond smiling coyly.

"Bartender, the same thing again. You're kind of nice Marie", said Roger turning to her. "You always work here . . . I mean, is this your steady job?"

"For the time bein'", said the blond as she tilted her glass to her mouth and emptied half of it. "Excuse me a minute, will ya?" she said, touching Roger's arm. "Joanie, Joanie, come here a minute, will ya?" she called toward the end of the bar.

From the corner where the girls had been sitting, came Joanie, a short, plump, in a sensual way, sandy-haired girl.

"Don't you think you should introduce your friend, Charlie, and Joanie. She looked so lonely over there, . . . and Charlie is all by himself, too", said Marie to Roger as Joanie joined them.

"Charlie, this is Joannie . . . I'm Roger, Joannie", Roger shook her hand. Charlie walked around Roger, put his arm around her waist and guided her to his far side. "Bartender . . ."

"Let's have a celebration toast", said Marie.

"What'll we celebrate?" said Roger.

"We'll celebrate all of us being together, how's that?" Roger and Charlie liked the idea.

"Teddy", called Marie.

The bartender came over and filled all the glasses.

"And now boys", the MC announced as she came in front of the curtain again, "we have a real special treat for you. She needs no introduction—Red Hot!"

The curtains started to open; the brassy little band in the recessed darkness of the stage started into one of its noisy, bumpy tunes.

"This ought to be pretty good", said Charlie, staring at the stage without turning around to Roger.

"Yeah", said Roger, who twisted toward the stage, leaning on the bar with his elbow, his back toward Marie. Joanie and Marie watched unconcernedly as Red Hot, covered completely in a flowing black cape, strutted on stage in time to the beat. The cape, as she turned around, could be seen to go up the back of her neck, forming a little cap behind her head. Red Hot danced and cavorted around the stage, in time with the music, twirling occasionally so that her legs, right up to the skimpy g-string covering her lower torso would show beneath the lifting material. She turned, with her back to the gaping men, opened the front of the cape and twirled back again. The cape slid off her shoulders. Catching it in her hand as it fell, she now stood clad in only a red mesh bra and g-string. Red Hot turned her back again to the bulgyeyed patrons, and as she did, she hooked the black cape with its little cap on the middle of her bra so that it covered the front of her body. Red Hot began to skip around the stage, and when she reached the front, facing the hypnotized audience, that black cape didn't look like a black cape any more. It resembled the shadow of a man, clinging to her body, the cap was his head, the cape his back.

The music started again in a slow booming rhythm, and Red Hot danced with her arms around her imaginary lover, clasping him to herself. She twisted and twirled, and the cap assaulted her body with imaginary kisses. Red Hot twisted her head to escape the imaginary kisses. Slowly, as her body pulsated to the beat, the cape began slowly to slide lower on her body until the cap was lodged at a level in the hollow between her breasts. She twisted languorously, the cap now covered one of her breasts. Her lover was devouring one of her breasts; and she twisted and contorted with contrived delight. Her entire body was pulsating, but she remained in the same spot twisting away from and holding her lover at the same time. Then her dusky lover assaulted her other breast as she twisted her upper body. The cap twisted center again, and Red Hot pushed both breasts behind the cap.

"Roger, would you buy us another drink?", said Marie from behind Roger's back.

"Hunh . . . oh, yeah, sure . . . the money is on the bar", he motioned to the bartender, ... "get them another . . ." said Roger, never taking his eyes off the twisting, cavorting body and her imaginary lover who, now aided by the pulsations, slid down further on Red Hot's body. Red Hot was gritting her teeth in feigned ecstasy. The cap lodged now at a spot at between her thighs. Red Hot was standing on the stage, with the little band beating a constant rhythm . . . boomba . . . boomba . . . boom, her arms extended above her head, her body twisting, pushing, sliding against her imaginary lover's head with each beat. She now bit one of her arms with the sheer ecstasy of her dance gyrating her torso to the brass booming of the band.

Roger and Charlie were mesmerized, motionless, staring at the stage, their drinks suspended in their hands. Joanie and Marie chatted with each other, sipping their drinks occasionally.

The brassy music stopped. Red Hot continued gyrating her hips in the middle of the stage; then she emitted a scream which shattered the stillness of the bar. She grabbed and pulled her hair in excruciating delight. Red Hot straightened up and smiled at the audience. Weak applause filtered forward.

Red Hot gripped the flimsy material of her mesh g-string and drew it aside quickly letting it snap back into place and walked off the stage.

Roger and Charlie kept staring at the stage as the curtains closed, swayed in place and were still. Charlie turned around and looked at Roger who was facing him. His eyes widened.

"Ever see that in Tylersville, Roger?" Charlie was virtually astounded.

"No, no I didn't", Roger said slowly. "I think she's wasting time with that dummy, though", said Roger, as he laughed leeringly. "C'mon girls have another drink", he said finally.

Marie and Joanie perked up and slid their glasses forward for another round.

"Let's get a table", suggested Joanie. "We could be more chummy that way".

"Nah, . . . we aren't going to stay that long", said Charlie.

"How come", said Roger, "we're doin' alright right here".

"Yeah, c'mon", chimed in Marie, holding Roger's arm. "We'll have some laughs".

"No, we can't Rog. We've got that other place to go to", said Charlie, trying to catch Roger's eyes.

"Okay, Charlie", Roger shrugged, "you're the boy tonight".

"We'll have one more round", said Charlie, "and then we'll go, okay? C'mon girls, drink up".

Both Roger and Charlie were a little high as they hailed a cab outside the bar.

"Why couldn't we stay there?", asked Roger, swaying in the headlights of the approaching cab.

"Because—here, let's grab this cab . . . I'm going to show you an even better place", said Charlie as he jumped into the back compartment of the cab. "The Brummel Club, up on forty eight street please", said Charlie, as Roger sat next to him. Roger slammed the door and settled back into the seat.

"We shoulda stayed there", said Roger looking out the window on his side of the cab, "those girls were all right, . . . especially that little Marie".

"Naw, they just drink your booze, . . . and that table action, three and a half bucks per person just to sit down. That's all they want you to do is sit at one of those crummy tables. They'll bring out all kinds of crap bubbly wine, and you pay like hell for it. You notice these dames keep drinkin' and don't get drunk? The bartender must give them watered drinks. I always figure they're making money on every drink they make you buy, and then they hustle off home, leaving you holding the bill. Besides, they work until four o'clock. What the hell are we, owls?" Charlie laughed at his own words.

"Yeah, owls", repeated Roger laughing. "Where the hell are we going now?" Roger looked at Charlie.

"What's the difference?", said Charlie throwing his head back. "Your wife and family aren't here to keep check on you. This is our night to howl . . . yaahhooo", screamed Charlie.

"Hey, Mac, you want to keep it a little more quiet", said the cab driver, looking at Charlie through his rear view mirror. "A cop'll stop us and give me a ticket".

"Shhh, Charlie, you wouldn't want our chauffeur to get a ticket, would you?" asked Roger lightly.

"No, Sir, not me", answered Charlie lurching himself upright with the aid of the strap hanging from the side of the cab, looking out the window. "This is the spot, . . . this is it, right here. Hold it", Charlie said impatiently to the driver.

"Take it easy, Mac, take it easy. You'll get there", said the driver.

Roger looked past Charlie—who was taking money out of his pocket—to the spot in front of which they had stopped. A small canopy, a door, and a small picture window to the side of the door was all he could see.

"Here you go driver. Keep it", said Charlie, handing the driver a bill.

"What is this place?", said Roger as he followed Charlie out of the cab. "It looks dead".

"Don't worry about dead", said Charlie putting his hand up to stifle all fears, "don't worry about a thing. Ol' Charlie is the Captain of this ship", he jabbed his chest with his thumb.

"Did you say Captain of this shit?" said Roger smiling.

"Ship, . . . ship. You know I wouldn't say shit, you know that, Roger, old buddy", said Charlie as he laughed.

They walked into the little bar. A girl, who was sitting at the end of the bar, disentangled a male friend's hand from her waist and came over to them.

"Hello Charlie, . . . how're you tonight?", she said as she took his coat.

"Okay, Arlene", he said looking around the room. "This is Roger. Is Mary here?"

Arlene nodded. "Yeah, she's in the back. Here's your coat check Charlie". "Oh thanks. C'mon Roger".

"Hold it a second", Roger called to Charlie as he took off his coat.

Roger made his way to the back of the bar where Charlie was ordering a drink. This was a plush, subdued place, with dark walls, a bar against one wall, and a dining alcove with ten or twelve tables in the back, a piano in the middle of the alcove. An older, colored woman was playing the piano and singing some supper-club blues. Beyond the dining alcove was a stairway to a lower floor.

"Well, what's the big attraction here?" asked Roger. "There's hardly anyone here".

"Take it easy Roger, you'll see in a minute, . . . two scotch and sodas", said Charlie to the bartender.

Standing further forward at the bar were a couple of men, a girl, and at the far end, a couple of other men, and Arlene, the coat check girl. From some place behind the back wall of the bar came a heavy-set, buxom woman with black hair, clad in a low-cut dress which gave an unobstructed view of her huge bosom, thereby negating any detraction her heaviness might make. She recognized Charlie and walked toward him.

"Hello Mary, how's the girl?" said Charlie, smiling.

"Hello, Charlie. How've you been?", she asked as she put her arms around him in a friendly embrace. "Where you been keepin' yourself?" she said still embracing him, looking into his face.

"Oh, I've been pretty busy. Roger, say hello to Mary".

"Hello", said Mary. "Glad to meet a friend of Charlie's anytime", she said as smiled at Roger. "So what's cookin'?" she said to Charlie.

"That's what we came to see", said Charlie.

"Have a drink. Buy the boys a drink on me", she said to the bartender. "Have to make a couple of phone calls. I'll be back in a minute". She walked to the area behind the back wall and disappeared.

"What's going on?" asked Roger.

"Shhh", said Charlie winking at Roger. "You I'll see".

As the two of them stood with drinks at the bar, a woman came into the bar. She was well dressed, with light hair, about thirty-five years old. She walked further into the room, looking at the people seated on the stools by the bar. The bartender behind the bar was keeping pace with her as she walked. As she approached the man sitting next to Roger, the bartender motioned to her.

"Right here", he said.

The woman stopped and slipped in between Roger and the man on the stool next to him. "Hello", she said to the man.

"Hello", the man smiled widely, moving off his stool. "I've been expecting you. Sit down won't you?" He offered her his stool, and he slipped over to the next one. "What would you like to drink?"

"A scotch old fashioned", she said as she slipped off her long black gloves, and let her coat drop onto the back rest of the stool.

Mary came out of the back room and walked over to Charlie. As she was about to speak, she saw the woman who had just come in. A slight smile rippled across her lips.

"Excuse me a minute", Mary said to Charlie. She turned to the woman. "Hi. How'd you know just where to go?" she asked with a delighted smile on her face.

"I can always pick out a handsome man when I see one", she said playfully. "You said he was handsome, didn't you?" The three of them laughed.

Roger looked toward Charlie with a quizzical look. Charlie winked.

"Say, Mary", said Charlie. "Do you think you could get a date for Roger and myself? You must know a couple of girls in town who would want to go out with two nice looking guys like us".

Mary pursed her lips and narrowed her eyes in mock consideration, then nodded. "I think I have just the girls you would like". Mary looked toward the door as two girls entered the bar. "Stay here a minute", she said as she prodded Charlie's arm to stay him.

"Hello Gina, Fran, how're you?", Mary said as the two girls were unfastening their coats. "Come this way", she said, indicating the direction with a slight jerk of her head. She started walking toward the back, past Charlie on whose arm she put her hand again. "I'll be right with you, honey".

The two girls followed Mary until they all reached one of the tables in the back where three men were seated. The men rose. Mary made introductions and the two girls sat down. Mary made her way back toward Charlie and Roger. Behind her, a waiter walked to the table to take an order from the girls.

"I think I have just the girls for you. I'll call them in a few minutes. They went out a while ago, and I know they're not home yet. Can you wait a few minutes?"

"Sure, sure", answered Charlie.

"Mary", called the bartender; as he motioned to the phone.

"What do you say Rog? Can we wait around a few minutes to have some fun?"

"Suppose we can", said Roger, not really sure if what he thought was happening, was happening.

Mary walked behind the bar and took the phone receiver from the bartender. "Hello, . . . who?" she said straining her ears against the noise of the room. She put the index finger of her free hand in her ear. "Well, gee, I don't think I can see you tonight. I'm pretty tied up right now. Uhh, yes, I think so. Maybe we can make it soon". She listened for a moment. "And thanks for keeping me in mind. Sure. What? Okay. Bye". She hung up the phone and came back to Roger and Charlie.

"Pretty busy tonight, eh?", said Charlie.

"Just regular. Pretty quiet now, but it was busy before. Probably get busy again later".

Two men walked in and handed their coats to the hat-check girl. Mary walked over to them; they talked a while, and then walked to the back and sat at a table. As they were being seated, a lone girl walked in. Mary caught her eye with a wave of her hand, and the girl walked toward the back. Mary spoke to her and walked with her to the table with the three men and two girls. The waiter took her order, as Mary walked back toward the bar.

"Phil", Mary said to the man sitting next to Roger in a bit louder than conversational tone, "aren't you going to buy Claudia some dinner?"

Phil looked at Claudia; she gave an affirmative nod.

"Yeah, sure Mary, get us a table will you?" he said laughing. "Don't want to starve this lovely creature". The girl remained unaffected by the compliment. Perhaps growing accustomed to meaningless compliments bandied about, presumably to impress or arouse, by people that she came in contact with in her line, they no longer meant anything to her. As well they might not. A man buys pleasure, and yet wishes to feel that it is given to him because of love, by the most gorgeous of women.

"Did you know, Claudia just told me she was in Paris recently, Mary?", the man said as Mary led them to a back table. "Probably the same time I was. Too bad we didn't know each other then", he said taking the girls arm. "Did you see the new show that opened in that theater on the Champs Elysee? . . . oh, what the hell is the name of it?", continued the conversation, fading from earshot as the couple reached the back of the dining alcove.

As Mary started forward, she made a quick snapping motion of her fingers as she looked up and saw Charlie. She walked to the back of the bar and picked up the phone and dialed a number. She spoke briefly. When she was finished, she made her way back to Charlie and Roger, a hint of a smile on her lips.

"Called two nice girls for you. They said they'd be over in a few minutes, okay?"

"Great. Okay Roger?"

"Sure, sure thing. Great by me".

As Roger and Charlie stood at the bar, other men, mostly in twos and threes, came in. Mary seemed to know most of them. They ordered drinks and stood at the bar, talking amongst themselves or with other customers they knew. In a short while, the entire bar was filled with men and a couple of women. Men stood in a second row, and against the wall opposite the bar. A couple of girls walked in and room was made for them to sit on stools at the bar. In seconds, their stools were surrounded by vultures about their prey, except it seemed the vultures were really the prey begging to be chosen by the prey.

The two most recently arriving girls were different from the rest of the girls that were already in the bar. Those already there were usual, not common, looking women, representing all types, secretary-looking, sisterly, friendly, all different, yet all sharing in one thing; they were conservative, neatly dressed, not looking to make themselves stand out. The two new-comers were different; they looked hard. One had red hair, the other black. Both wore their hair long, and both had off-the-shoulder dresses. They had hard, coarse looks; their make-up was heavy, over-stated. They sat and drank, and talked to the men who surrounded them, twisting occasionally from one to the other. One of the men next to the redhead slid one hand, knuckles inward, into the upper part of her dress, pulling it away from her body, peering as he did in order to see what treasure the material hid. The redhead lurched back, her movement removing the hand from her dress.

The fellow was persistent. "C'mon, just a little peek", he said, slipping his hand inside her dress again.

"You gonna stop or do I hit you in the head with this glass?" she said, gritting her teeth behind closed lips as she looked self-consciously to see if others were watching.

The fellow stepped back and with head cocked to one side, surveyed her body as she sat on the stool. His gestures were mostly for affect, to impress the girl and the rest at the bar how calculating and, therefore, how experienced he was at this sort of thing. He was surveying her legs, her rear end. Someone touched his shoulder. It was Mary. She said something to him, pointing to the back, where a girl who had just come in was standing. He put his glass down on the bar and kissing the redhead on the temple, walked to the table area.

The redhead made a face and turned to the fellow who was standing on the other side of her and began talking.

"Boy, this is some place", said Roger. "There's an awful lot of guys here. What is the big attraction? There aren't many girls".

"More'll come in later. I guess when they leave their sugar daddies and boyfriends off they come out to have some real fun. You have enough money with you Roger? I mean, you can charge it to your expense account, of course, but you have cash with you, don't you?"

"I have fifty bucks. That should be enough, no?"

"Yeah, yeah. We can have a meal here—I think the girls save their appetite for when they meet guys like us. It's cheaper for them. Then we'll go out somewhere, not late, you have to get that plane in the morning. Probably only need thirty, forty at the most, something like that".

Roger shrugged.

"What the hell man", said Charlie, "live it up. You don't get away from Fran and home that often do you?"

"You're right about that", agreed Roger, with a grave nod of the head. "We'll really live it up tonight. No worries about the house, or the wife, or the daughter, or the anything". Just then, Roger remembered the scene in the living room the other night, remembered Nancy and her would-be lover. He hoped that Francine, his wife, would be vigilant. Never know what happens to a nice girl these days.

"Roger, Charlie . . . this is Marie, and Joan". Mary was standing next to their table with two girls. One had light colored hair, worn down to the shoulder. The other had dark hair, closely cropped in a dutch-boy hair style.

"Well, well", said Roger, standing to offer his chair, "sit down, sit down. What lovely girls you picked", he said quickly to Mary, "Couldn't have picked nicer if I did it myself".

Charlie looked at Roger quizzically. The girls sat.

"Want a drink, girls?" asked Charlie.

"I'll have a scotch and soda," said Joan who was the light-haired girl, now sitting next to Roger.

"I'll have a martini", said Marie.

"A martini, a scotch and soda, a scotch and water here, and another scotch and soda there", Roger said to the waiter.

"Do you fellows come in here often?" asked Marie.

"Well, I come in every once in a while. My friend is from out of town", said Charlie.

"Oh?", said Joan, "here on business?"

"You might say that", answered Roger with a leer in his voice. Charlie and the girls laughed.

"Why don't we order something to eat now, so that we can get quick service and get out of here?" said Joan.

Roger and Charlie felt a jolt of masculine ego shudder through them. How strange that the men thought the women wanted to get out quickly so that they might be with them all the quicker. It would never become apparent that the girls wanted to get the evening's work over with so they could go home to bed—alone. Men have odd notions about women. They are complimented if even the slightest tramp wants them. A man is complimented, is a conqueror. A woman is offended, is conquered. A man is a lover, a woman a tramp, and all stemming from one and the same action. And yet, does not a woman also long for the warmth of a relationship as much as a man.

"Good idea", smiled Charlie.

They ordered dinner, and as the night drew on, they finished their drinks, their dinner, and left the bar and completed their sordid, calculated business.

It was afternoon now, and the sun reflected from the silvery wings as it does from the glistening ocean on a July day, with the waves lapping at the edge of the beach drawing sand away, then returning it, then drawing it away, then returning it, then drawing . . . Roger was being lulled to sleep by his own thoughts. His eyelids seemed to have a magnetic attraction for each other. They kept slipping over his orbs, trying to shut him off from the people seated about him; from the sign that lit up NO SMOKING, from the silver wings, from the people standing on the observation platform being blown by the breeze but staying to wave to their loved ones, from the silvery wings with the bouncing fire, from the greyish circle on the forewing where the propellers were spinning . . .

I'm tired, Roger thought to himself. He had left Charlie only a few hours ago, left him at the hotel, and now he was on his way home. They hadn't even taken off, yet his eyelids started to close again, and his head started to droop down toward his chest . . . lower, lower, then it nodded slightly as he caught himself and raised his head. His eyes sleepily, half closed peered about him . . .

Glad I don't come on these trips often, he thought. *Lord knows, I couldn't take it . . . be good to get home and get some sleep . . . tell Francine I had a late session trying to settle some business matters. Maybe I'll tell her I couldn't sleep all night worrying about her and Nancy. No, I couldn't tell her that.* Roger's head started to nod again. *Nancy*, he thought as his eyelids began to close. *Have to talk to her again. Don't want anything to happen to her. My only child, my Princess. I want her to have everything nice. God!* he said waking himself with the thought and raising his head, *I'd never let my daughter go to New York alone. You can never tell what might happen to her. Jesus, that whole bar was full of hungry guys last night, each one out for all he could get, not caring what happens. What the hell, I don't make a habit of it. And, anyway, the girl I was with was a whore, probably does that sort of thing every night, maybe twice a night. I only get to town once in a while—what the hell. But those guys in New York, they're different, they're rotten, smart alecks, take out after any girl, any kind of a girl, any one they see, anytime they can.* Roger's eyes were almost completely closed. *What a rotten hole of a city, full of whores and perverts . . . glad it's not like that back home. At least you can raise a nice family and live a clean wholesome life, without any of this scum. Got to try and tell Nancy.* His head nodded lower, lower, raising up again *Got to keep her away from all the filth in this filthy world.* Roger's head slumped downward again, but this time he did not raise it. The engines spun faster, the plane skimmed across the runway, lifting toward home. Within, Roger slept the sleep of a man resting from the exertions of a business trip.

MARGARITA

Perhaps because of the cinema, one always thinks of funerals wilting beneath anguished skies pouring rain. Yet, as Margarita's coffin slowly lowers, sun glints from its bronzed surface. The graveyard is alive with graceful trees, the breeze scented with a sweet newly mown pungency. Concentration is difficult at a funeral. One feels a necessity for solemnity, but many thoughts about the departed and the past are interspersed and juxtaposed with distractions, and one feels guilty for this lack of solemn bereavement.

As I gaze down, my head lowered in silence and reverie, the summer morning heat warms my bent neck, beads of perspiration on my forehead, and turns the half moist, recently unearthed dirt from dark chocolate to dry cocoa. My eyes are distracted by my hands throbbing involuntarily by palsy at my sides. I would like to stop their irreverent trembling, for I feel not only old because of them, but embarrassed. But, then, not many people will notice the feebleness of an old man.

A sprightly black dot in the air drones and flies whimsically in front of me, distracting me again. I lift my eyes to follow his frivolous flight. He darts down to the moist dug earth, alighting on a rocky mound. Distracted again, I scan the length of the green field dotted with man shaped stones. A barred fence keeps the progress and hectic activity and confusion of the world at bay, so the sleeping can absorb sublime peacefulness and beauty.

Beyond the fence I see children hopping and skipping, playing together in their youthful joy. How lovely little children are! I recall Margarita as a child. I was young and unshaking then. She was younger yet, much younger, with black hair flowing to her shoulders, and small square child's teeth glistening in her full child's face. She was a lovely child, flowing with activity and fun, asking questions in quest of knowledge about this grand world into which she was growing. I remember when Margarita lost a front tooth. The gaping hole in her mouth was black and disfiguring, but this only added to her delightful appearance. When she smiled, she made you smile. Children, especially little girls, are wonderful creatures filled with joy and hope and anticipation, so enjoyable for themselves.

Margarita grew to be a graceful girl. She grew quite pretty, with dark, dark eyes, and darker hair. Her adult teeth were not as evenly aligned as they should have been, but even this did not detract from her charm. As she grew older, Margarita was still always laughing and happy, cheering even the most dismal hours of those around her. Her very existence seemed to fill the lives of those about her. I witnessed all the years of her aging. I, too, was aging, but she helped the tiredness and frustration of life disappear with her laughter.

I can remember her as she was then, her almost mature body swaying provocatively. It was amazing to see this once little ball of giggly laughter become a soft, undulating almost-woman with a haunting laugh. True, she did not become the most beautiful woman, but she always had an irresistible effect on me. The years flow back so easily now, without order or sequence. They've passed so silently. I almost forget they are gone . . . until I feel my hands shaking.

Margarita grew older, and it was a joy to see her becoming aware of life, or blossoming into womanhood, tasting the joys of being youthfully alive. She began to go out with young men, not really men yet, and how handsome she thought they were, and what great and grave aspirations they had. She was very happy. Often, though, the young men made her sad too. They came into and passed out of her life with despairing silence, and she would be tearful and full of sorrow.

After a strange thing occurs, it is difficult to recall and trace its origin. Strangely and ever so slowly, Margarita changed. Not that everyone would notice at a glance. But one who had watched her grow, had watched her gay laughter, could notice hardness in her face, straight rough lines surrounding her mouth, her laughter now harsher. Who knew why it had come? Perhaps it was just an almost grown woman's way of frustration with her young men, I thought at the time. But it grew worse, and it was frightening. I made sincere offerings of friendship and companionship, which she threw down unceremoniously. It made me sad. Not that she wouldn't accept my offering, but that I couldn't help her.

She began to talk with men, not boys any longer. She did not want to be bothered with boys. When she was old enough, to the heartache of her mother, she would sit in a bar, not in a booth or anything ladylike, but actually at the bar with men of her acquaintance. Men, lonely and bitter men, who had a propensity to stay out of their own homes, and who enjoyed her youthful, female companionship. It was agonizing to see such a delicate flower amidst human debris. She was headstrong and wild, and would not listen to anyone. Her eyes would flash with anger, and her white teeth would glisten as they were bared in defense of her loose independence. Her mother suffered because of this wildness. She ached and worried and tried to appease Margarita's wild spirits, but to no avail. Margarita became more strange, more bitter, more intense in her worldliness.

I remember a party. I stepped out of the house in which the party was held, in need of fresh air and a cigarette. Standing in the dark, clear night, looking into the sky, I head a noise. It was a vague sort of noise, a rustle, a sigh. I turned and saw Margarita. Not that I really saw her, but I saw a couple leaning together in a darkened doorway, tightly embracing. It was she, her dark long hair hanging over the man's shoulder, stealing love. Silently I went back to the party. She returned later, saying she had gone for a walk by herself. I, if no one else, or perhaps it is just that like I, they did not say anything, noticed the faded mark of her smeared lipstick over-reaching her lips.

A detestation of her adult irreverence for the spirit of her innocence made me hate her then. I wanted to grab her by her hair and twist her into the ground. My insides ached with anger, but I said nothing. Her paramour, a married man, an ugly, sensual man, came back a few minutes later. He, I hated more. I wanted to murder him right there and then . . . but to what end? Was it his fault? Would that end it? If I had been sure that it would, I would happily have killed him. I remained silent and motionless. They party continued its strange cycle.

Margarita left home soon after that, and I saw her very little. When I did see her, and I hated the very thought of what she represented, the agony she brought to her mother. One day that good soul asked me to look for Margarita and bring her home where she belonged. I did. I found her living in a cheap rooming house, in a room filled with junky trinkets and cheap furniture, a thick fragrance of cheap perfume permeating the air. She was steady eyed, her jaw formed in challenge . . . but the fire had gone out of her eyes. They were dull and lifeless. She would not yield, and threw back in my teeth, the entreaty of her mother.

I raged and vented hatred for her until my voice gave out, but she was uncaring and emotionless. I wanted to throttle her. It was a feeling of utter loathing that filled my being. It was hard to tell her mother the coarse things that Margarita had said . . . and it was harder for that mother to accept the absence of Margarita. That mother who had nursed her, her first party, her first prom, that woman who took such delight in the most simple activity of her daughter, was now shunted aside to some ill remembered corner of the past.

Not long afterward, Margarita's mother died. It was a sad funeral, sadder because it was not well attended, noted mostly for the absence of the daughter. It did not rain that day either. My hatred of the girl began to turn to pity for her worthless existence. She was harsh, and I was reconciled.

I saw Margarita alive only once after that. A short while ago, when she was ill, just before her death. I was summoned, although I can't imagine how they knew to contact me. Now I am so old, so useless, so hardly able to help myself . . . but I agreed to go. Even in my contempt there was not a callousness. My legs drag slowly after my body now, and my arms shake, but for Margarita . . . wonderful, laughing, bright eyed Margarita, asking her childhood questions, I made the effort.

I found her in a bed. It was supposed to be a bed, covered with slick and dark-with-dirty sheets, in a room of pale green, and cracked plaster, a dripping sink against one wall, and a cardboard closet with cheap clothes and stockings hanging from the back of a spare wooden chair. She lived with a man there. He was filth, like the surroundings, filthy, rotten and hateful, degrading, his eyes haunted with drink, skinny, dirty clothes, hard working and ignorant. Cheap pulp romance books were strewn about the room.

Oh, God, how I regret that day. How I wish these eyes had gone blind, that I had ended my existence before I walked up those flights of stairs and entered that room. She looked at me almost unknowingly. Her eyes looked as if they were eaten away. There was nothing there, just dots, not dark, but milky brown, her hair was stringy, her skin pale and ugly.

She recognized me, perhaps, before she died. She smiled a little, just ever so faintly, and I could look back instantly on her youthful days. I could hear her long ago laughter, her bright smiling child's face, filled with glistening child's teeth. She had just a little smile left now. Just a very little.

She died with that little smile on her face. Quietly, without a sound, she left this life of which she had tasted both good and foul. She lay there dead, silence pounding pressure against my ears. Suddenly I almost wept. I could feel that slightly burning, slightly expanding sensation around my eyes. I could feel pressure in my nose. I thought I had outgrown weeping. I thought I had wept all my tears at my wife's funeral. But there were more . . . many more.

And now, the sun glinting off the casket as it slowly lowers, I can feel the welling of tears around my eyes. What a strange life. I cannot despise the girl. I want to wipe the tears, but I am embarrassed for my hands. I just lift my head and gaze out over the field again, drops of water rolling slowly down my face.

Blurredly I see the children outside still playing . . . wonderful children . . . reminding me somehow of my lovely, lovely, little daughter Margarita. The casket is in the hole, but somehow my life is not as shattered as at the parting of my wife. I look around at the peaceful trees, the sweet smelling lawn . . . it is not that I love her less, but that soon we three will all be together, at peace, again.

THE TRIP

I do not know when the inception for this scheme, which I am now in the process of fulfilling, came to be. I know not where or when or how or why. Perhaps in a hypnologic state of dazedness my clever and diabolical mind touched upon the idea in fantasy, or in a morose daydream of self-destruction I summoned, to my detriment, this weird plan, or perhaps in the unsteadiness of a venture with potent fermentation. No matter, . . . for now, whatever the reason for the inception, I find myself seated behind the steering wheel of an old, battered automobile, too old and unwanted in this present state of glittering fancy to be worth much to anyone. Anyone except me, who am about to use it to start a series of events which will ultimately lead to my becoming hundreds of thousands of dollars richer. Yes, I am going to use this car as a pawn in a game of wits, a game wherein the players know not yet they are playing, or at least the other players in the game do not know they are playing. I, as one of the players, have certainly devoted immoderate time and energy and thought and worry on this little game, on the strategy to be employed, on the *modus operandi*, to be well aware of the circumstances, to be well aware of the dangers involved, of the chances necessary, and of the ultimate success of my plan. I am quite sure that my plan is perfect, and without defect . . . and yet, . . . and yet, in my heart, an uneasiness is rocking nervously, quivering, warning me of failure, trembling with trepidation. Yet I go on. I must go on. I will not allow myself to desist. Am I trying to destroy myself? I do not know. I cannot think of that now. I have not the time for subtle and vague reflections. The only reflection I can be conscious of at this moment is the reflection of the road behind me in the mirror above my head. You'll notice of course, that even in the brightness of mid-day, this road is not overly crowded. Oh, an occasional car passes by on its way to the highway, but other than that, this part of the road, right here by all the wharves and docks, is not very traveled or peopled. As a matter of fact, I have a favorite spot on the end of one of the wharves where many pleasant hours of reflections and meditations have been lulled by the sibilant rolling of the waves against the pilings of the wharf. Conscious of reflections again, I gaze up into the rear view mirror. The road behind me is bare and sun drenched, with slight pools of dust, a glistening spectrum colored in the downbeating rays of the sun. A car is turning the corner, having on its metallic joints, and twists toward me. This is not he for whom we are waiting. The car rolls closer, the engine becoming droningly audible, and then it passes, whooshing the wind behind it, and again, I am alone, looking at the road. There really is no necessity for worry or apprehension or anxiety about the truck coming. I have approximately four minutes to wait, . . . four, perhaps five, . . . perhaps six, . . . but no more, . . . no more than six minutes from now a truck, not an ordinary truck, but a tow truck, will lumber heavily and powerfully around that corner, and roll toward the highway. It will not be just an ordinary unordinary tow truck either, for it will be the tow truck of the Allied Armored Car Corporation. No, not an armored car, just a tow truck for armored cars. Another of, shall I say, the pawns in this little game. As I've already said I cannot remember the exact instant I conceived this plan, but it has been boiling and heaving in my cranium for the better part of two weeks. Not too long a time for a man to become hundreds of thousands of dollars richer, you say? Quite true, by ordinary standards; but then, were I an ordinary man I would not be planning this little adventure. That's what it is, you know, an adventure. A scheme which is designed to bring to my otherwise, and unfortunately so, serene life, some excite-ment. Life is so, shall I say, tiring that I find myself constantly in quest of adventures, dreams which fill the void of this existence, mystifica-tions which form the more memorable aspects of my life, the while I wait for the somber morticians in their ebon suits, whose dreary step I hear already echoing on my doorstep, the while I wait for him who is to cover my dirt with more dirt, to come and carry me away. Do I sound like an old man, waiting for death. No not really. I am quite young, as successful young businessmen are measured. I'm thirty-two. No matter. I was telling you of how I initiated this cabal for becoming richer. No, that is most certainly not quite accurate. Let me start out from the beginning, as one should always start, with a proper notion of the entire scheme of things, and through diligence, observation, and planning, surmount each step correctly so that when the end of our trip is reached, we need not even look back to check if we have made a mistake. This following then, is the "how" I have schemed my little schema, which I have just begun to correctly state. I started not only, mind, I did not say not at all, but rather, not only, not only with the idea of becoming rich, that is rather nice, but also with the idea that in undertaking this scheme I would enjoy very much the thrill of this battle of wits. A noble battle of honor and wits fought with the staid and very tried and true conventionalities of that most protective and most sacred and most carefully guarded protector of the com-monwealth, the armored car.

This conveyance of wealth is shielded all around with thick armor, so that one cannot shoot the men inside, and therefore stop them from their appointed rounds—no that's the Post Office. At any rate, this in-genious machine was designed with thieves in mind, ordinary petty, bungling thieves, that is, for any thief who would plunder by killing and butchering, by force of arms, is really a peasant at heart. You see, the entire game I have designed, takes only my wits and myself into play; and I intend by the sagacious manipulation of my powers, to outwit this rumbling, moving fortress, with a swift and delicate thrust at its underside. This challenge involved, of course, was certainly one of the main considerations in the selection of this particular plan and this particular method of, shall I say, disregarding the distinctions between "meum et tuum". It is not the money so much, just as it is never the battle, but to have fought well; that is fruition.

I imagine that on one of my forays to the end of the wharf, which is right down there, you see, behind that parked truck trailer, you see the cleat by the edge of the warehouse, well just behind that, there is a lip on which you can walk to the end of the wharf. No one stops you of course, since the warehouse and wharf have been unused now for six weeks. And I've checked, naturally I've checked everything, and it will not be operational again for at least another week. That trailer truck will be parked there for two more days, then it will leave for Chicago. It comes in rather handy too, as you shall see. There have been left no accidental aspects to this intrigue, for it is the overlooked in laziness which will spring up suddenly in revolt and foil a plot. Hmm, four more minutes to go, I'll have to outline this little maneuver rapidly, but let it suffice to say that on one of my trips to the end of the wharf, to my pallet of meditation, I decided, after passing the Allied Armored Car Corporation garage, or rather, I should say, I unconsciously filed the thought away for future meditation, that it would certainly be interesting to think of a way to outwit the steeled guardian and conveyor of the people's funds. I have often thought afterward that it was a devilish idea to contemplate since, in actuality, it could be very outrageous and harmful to the emotional stabilities of the stable. But then, by the same token, perhaps it was time they were stirred and prodded from their lethargy into doing something a bit more positive about their own protection. Nevertheless, the idea persisted and kept popping up at the most inopportune times, even once when I was in the presence, the, shall I say, quite charming presence, of a lovely young lady, . . . but that's another story. And we do not have time for rambling. Finally, I began to think of exactly how I would crack open, I use this term only for an expression as opposed to a physical reality, how I would outwit this armored car. I did not consider the "why" I would outwit it, for I was sure they carried large sums of currency now and then, and I could find that out easily enough. I considered merely the game. How to do it, how to create the intrigue. Would I purposely cause the van to have an accident? No police and the like would stream around in no time at all. Perhaps puncturing a tire with a pellet from a rifle; possibly, but then you could miss and your chances would be ruined. I conjured up hundred of ideas; and each was promising; but each lacked something, or each had a drawback, or presented one danger or another, or showed one weakness or another. It was a difficult, but most enjoyable, mental exercise; and when I finally had decided upon a method, I had to then decide about the amount of money, and the time and the place I would appropriate it. This was more difficult, but that I did not want to become involved with, or known to, the people who operated the armored cars. And so, in order to find out their destinations and routes, I had to follow each truck as they toured on their route, and mark down the time and the place, and the approximate size of the load which they were carrying from each stop. This took a great deal of time and zeal and disguises, for each time I followed a truck, I would alter my appearance in some way. In some obvious way, so that the drivers, when talking amongst themselves, would not accidentally mention someone who resembled me. This untimely occurrence of course would have stopped the plan instantly in its first stages.

Let me digress to tell you that even now that you see me, I am disguised. I do not usually wear glasses as I do now, and I do not have quite so aquiline a nose. These clothes are not quite to my taste and are rather shabby to be sure. And when I walk, I shall walk with a limp and a cane, neither of which I rely upon in my ordinary gait. Nevertheless, whenever I followed a truck, I would disguise myself by donning something, or using something, that was quite conspicuous, determining, that if this one thing was conspicuous, then the rest of what I had with me would be unnoticed. On some occasions, I wore a ridiculous and big red hat, on others I stuffed my jacket with a pillow to give me the effect of a deformed hunchback. On another occasion I rode a bike with knicker bockers on; this was an ordeal, because I had to ride my bike to keep up with the truck, which was quite tiring. Once I even acted the part of a blind man, with my Russian wolfhound Marunata playing the part of the guide dog. To proceed; after a series of disguises and sorties, I decided that the Bank of the Manufacturers Trust Company might be perfect. Are you familiar with the branch of this bank that is on 18th Street and Fourth Avenue? Oh, no. Well, it's a bank; and what more is there to say. One day, very inconspicuously, I opened a bank account there under the name of Maurice Seigal, . . . not a very original name, but then, not a very original fellow, this Seigal, . . . rather dirty and unshaven with a definite foreign accent and smell of garlic, . . . but he was useful in determining how the guards from the armored car entered the bank and how they removed the money, their hands grasping rather perfunctorily the handle of their weapons in their holsters, feeling rather like western sheriffs, and playing their parts to the hilt, their eyes darting from side to side of their eye sockets as they walked to the door, and out to the truck where another guard was standing, his hand on his pistol, watching the crowds in the streets, . . . and especially a rather delightful young girl with the most exquisite and undulating . . . ah well, . . . even these guards had not bad taste, . . . but is it taste that makes one realize that the obviously magnificent is magnificent? At any rate, . . . the guards put the money in the truck and would drive away, . . . and it was as simple as that. Life is rather simple when one brushes aside the filigree of nonsense that surrounds it . . . The truck would after it left the bank, travel down to the East River Drive, . . . taking approximately three minutes to get to the highway. There is no worry of the guards stopping for coffee or hot dogs on this trip, . . . which is an occurrence I have had to sit through almost as many times as I followed those trucks. But with the money in the truck it was forbidden to stop. So this of course was very convenient and opportune to note precisely the time it took for the truck to get to the highway, since the route had to be direct and constant. Now I digress again for the sake of clarity. I determined which truck would carry the most money by the amount they took out of the bank in their cloth bags, . . . and of course the locations of the bank, not only in reference to its physical locale, which could either hamper or assist my plan, but also with the thought of people and business surrounding it that would use the bank facilities. I deemed it prudent to find a highly commercial area, but not so intense a commercial area as to be either crowded with people or to be so efficient as to use too many checks and nonnegotiable securities. Approximating as best I could, which method had always been quite accurate, I found that this particular bank handled nice, tidy sums of currency and each Thursday they transferred three hundred thousand dollars to another bank in the downtown area. I would have actually thought seriously of tampering with this other bank, but it was impossible to calculate when the truck would arrive since traffic—is almost overpowering at all times, and the truck might—become stuck in traffic and ruin all my plans. You'll see clearly in a moment exactly why precise timing was so important in this little plan of mine. Hmm, . . . to wait a few more minutes. I shall have to get out of this car in approximately two minutes and start fixing a flat on the rear tire of this car. You'll notice the car is already tilted at an angle, . . . I have already jacked the rear end, just to save time. That's how I'm going to stop the tow truck, you see. An old man, an old crippled man, begging for assistance, . . . how could these kindly truck drivers refuse . . . their conscience would bother them for months. Well, perhaps we can conceive of a driver who would pass an old man mercilessly, . . . but not easily when the old man is standing directly in front of the tow truck. He'd have to run him down, . . . an old crippled man. Notice also that this thoroughfare is only large enough for one truck or car to pass through, . . . now that I have this disabled car I'm sitting in blocking half the road. What purpose stopping the tow truck? Well, when I stop them, or rather when this decrepit creature stops them and walks around to the driver's side, leaning on the truck constantly for support so that they cannot drive away, when I, I mean he, moves to the side, . . . when he moves to the side, he will ask in very supplicating, oh most compassionate tones, that the driver should assist him. I won't print what our driver might say here, for it might be somewhat offensive to delicate eyes, . . . but, in a less bleeding tone, I will, after leaping on the running board, and pressing this small but very effective revolver in his direction . . . Oh he'll be alone, . . . he and the tow truck, . . . and me, of course. Forgive me if I dawdle a bit as I go through this, but I am thinking and rechecking as I explain to you, considering all the remote possibilities. Do you recall what I told you about not having to recheck my path. It's true. I doubt I have made any errors or mistakes, . . . but this same restless brain that drives me in quest of adventure also insists incessantly that it be active, . . . and therefore I consider again the plot since it would be inappropriate right now to be thinking of anything else but the tow truck and the armored car which is now stuck on the road somewhere up ahead. Oh yes, . . . I'm sure the van is stopped somewhere ahead on the highway, feeling very safe in the open sunniness of the roadway, with cars streaming by quickly, whooshing air behind them, and men laughing and smiling mockingly, in the vicious way men have, . . . and they say to each other, "boy, some guys could come over here with guns and they'd be sitting ducks in that truck", . . . they only contemplate this jokingly, for they would not be so timorous as to attack that truck, not with the drivers sealed in behind a bullet-proof enclosure, guns in their holsters, and a rifle on the wall, . . . further, the openness makes it even riskier, . . . for the police will be driving past often, . . . the police may even stop and ask if the guards need help, . . . and they'll reply no, the repair truck is on the way, . . . and the police will drive away, . . . or even if they stay there, it won't matter to the repairman as he fixes the truck. It will certainly add to the protectedness and the comfortableness of the driver and guards in the armored car. Now you understand that I know all of these things because I have foreordained the paths of all my pawns. Were you here early this morning during the slumber hours, . . . approximately one-thirty in the morning. Well unfortunately, very, very unfortunately, there was a nasty accident in front of the Allied Armored Car Corporation. Two cars collided, when one car turned and crossed over the path of the other car. It was quite an accident, . . . and thank goodness no one was hurt. They were old cars, . . . about as old as this one, so there was no great loss . . . but it certainly did stir up no little excitement in front of the garage. The night watchman, good soul, called the police. How fortunate for the drivers of those cars, one of which actually turned over, . . . that they were in front of a place from which they could make a phone call. At that dreary hour of the morning in this deserted area there are not very many people about, . . . nor are there many phones available. Nevertheless there was a great deal of noise and confusion, . . . and the night watchman, good fellow that I said he is, was hopping about, helping the two drivers out of the wrecks, . . . and in the midst of this pandemonium it was not very difficult for me to slip unnoticed inside the garage. You see the accident was not really an accident and it was not unfortunate for my purpose. It certainly looked like an accident though. I had bought the cars, and

had found two young men in a bar, . . . two not so bright, but very ava-
ricious young men in a bar, and hired them to stage an accident for the
sake of tests which the Consolidated Insurance Company was making.
We, . . . we the insurance company, that is, wanted to check on the vis-
ibility, and the ability to stop, and the force of impact, and the damage
to car and driver and all sorts of nonsensical and sundry other data
which I used to persuade my gloriously greedy youth that this was
very important and necessary investigation. I assured them that the
cars were well enforced with roll bars on the inside, . . . which are steel
bars that brace the top of the car to absorb the shock of impact as the
car turns over. And I further assured them that an additional hundred
dollars apiece, additional to the other hundred dollars apiece I had
already pressed into their absorbing hands, would be theirs if they
would cooperate in this humanitarian cause. They said, "Certainly Mr.
Malone", . . . and a very respectable Mr. Malone I was, an insurance
agent, clothed in a conservative suit and hat, and dark rimmed glasses
and a large profuse moustache. I escorted my collaborators to the
warehouse, . . . the one right over there, where I had the two cars
parked. I had bought these cars separately, at two very different and
very separated junk dealers, with two different disguises, and I had the
protective steel added in at two very different and also very separated
welding shops, with two additional disguises. It's not really that difficult to disguise a mechanic in a coverall with grease smeared on his
face. One had a cap, and one glasses, and one a brush moustache, and
one a cigar and a most disgusting habit of spitting punctuating, . . . so
much so that the man in the welding shop told him to refrain from his
expectoration, . . . he used different wording of course, but it approxi-
mated the meaning. So here were the cars and the night and the spot
and the plan and the drivers. The drivers would be able to distinguish
each other by little red lights that I had mounted behind the grill of
each car, . . . so as they rode at each other from opposite directions on
the street, they would be sure not to become involved with any inter-
loping other car. I told one, . . . a red-headed fellow, to turn up Corne-
lia Street, . . . that's the side street that immediately skirts the Allied
garage, . . . and I told the other fellow to drive right into the side of the
turning car. I was to be at the scene, camera in hand, to record with

pictures our results, and to write reports. The anxious youth were quite thrilled and happy and impatient, since no one had ever asked them to go out and wreck a car purposely, . . . and pay them two hundred dollars besides. Their pleasure was imposing . . . they were very happy to be of service to such a worthy cause. About another minute and a half I should say and the tow truck will be upon me. Now let me see, . . . ah yes, . . . these two cars were driven rapidly and were smashed into each other, . . . and the din was deafening, the roar resounding, . . . and the night watchman jumped in fright and ran to the street, which of course was my cue to enter the garage. Very quickly I went into the small office which was used by the dispatcher during the day and the night watchman at night and from which he had just run. Smoke was still rising from a cup filled with coffee. There was a time clock on a counter which was used to punch the time on index cards made up as record for each truck. This Allied Corporation is a very efficient corporation to be sure, . . . so efficient, that they knew always where their tucks were, and what time they should be back, and which truck was at which bank, and all sorts of information that was most helpful, and soon to be detrimental, to them. They were even so efficient as to have the cards already made out for the following day, with the number of the truck that was to be at each particular pick-up designation. This was of course so the mechanic during the day, could check over each truck when it came in from its daily run, and insure that nothing would go wrong with it the next day, . . . because, though the trucks were unassailable, it wasn't good policy to let them break down on the streets.

Number One Hundred and Seventy Four, was the number of the truck to be used for the Manufacturers Trust Company, Union Square Branch; was very convenient. I left the office, and passed to where the trucks were standing quietly, passively, slumbering in the shadowy dim light of the garage. As I passed across the garage I could hear the excitement of the crash that had just occurred outside, and in the distance the wail of police sirens stirring up the silent night. I'm sure the two boys in the cars were quite surprised to find no photographer, and though I didn't intend to puzzle them too much, I had to, for now they couldn't tell anyone anything except that they were conducting experiments for a Mr. Malone of the Consolidated Insurance Company. Everyone looked at them dazedly, I'm sure, and no one knew what was happening, no one except me, and I was inside and had lifted the cover from the motor compartment of truck #174, and had quickly pulled out the wire that runs from the coil to the distributor, or from the distributor to the coil, depending from which end you begin. This is the wire along which the electric charge of life for the engine runs constantly. Nevertheless, I pulled the wire, inserted a little mechanism I am quite proud to have invented, into the hole in the coil from which I had pulled the wire, and put the wire back in a similar hole in the top of this little mechanism. The little mechanism? Well, it was, and is, merely a sort of junction switch and timer. You see, the spark would travel across this switch just as it would across just the wire, but, . . . the timepiece was rigged like an alarm clock switch; at a predestinated hour it would release, noiselessly of course, and the switch would break the circuit, and no juice would pass from the coil to the distributor and then, of course, the truck would stop running. Rather cleverly simple, wouldn't you say? It took approximately ten seconds for me to install the device, and then I carefully closed the hood, and through a side window, checking first the street outside, I jumped to the ground and went home for a happy and relaxed night's sleep. Out in front of the garage all the people concerned were probably still scratching their heads with unknowingness; and the two boys felt duped, and were quite disappointed about their money. Since, though, I had told them I would give them another hundred dollars apiece, I mailed two crisp one hundred dollar bills from Grand Central Post Office to their addresses, which I had gained as information for the Consolidated Insurance Company.

The stage was now somewhat set. Knowing that the truck was to arrive at the bank at approximately 10:30 Ante Meridian, and that it took approximately five minutes to load the money into the van, and since it took approximately another three minutes for them to attain the highway, . . . therefore eight minutes from the time of their arrival, I set the timing mechanism on my little invention for 10:40, allowing two minutes just for the sake of safety. In the added two minutes, the truck could reach and drive onto the highway. It doesn't matter

to which point on the highway they drive since they couldn't possibly be any further away than across the lane as I approached with the
tow truck. Oh yes, I will be manning the tow truck. You see, after I
point the revolver at the driver, I persuade him to drive me to my
favorite warehouse, which as I've already noted has not been used for
many weeks, and to which I have made a key, and which is therefore
completely at my disposal, and which contains such sundry items as
I might need for this adventure. Items like rope, and tear gas? Well,
I'll tell you in a minute. At any rate, after I take the tow truck and
the tow truck driver into the warehouse, I bind the driver, not too
tightly of course, and lock him in an office. Then, out of his sight, I don
my grease monkey's suit, change my glasses for a bandage across the
bridge of a twisted nose, chomp on an Italian cigar, which I wouldn't
light for all the money in the world, and drive off to rescue the disabled
truck. Of course they would have called the garage for assistance; what
else were they to do, push the truck, or leave it there? No! Allied has
a remarkably rapid and efficient repair service, for obvious reasons. It
is quite a large force of repair trucks, and repairmen, which of course
also adds facility to my effort to appear as a new hired man, and with
grease on my face, and a conspicuous bandage, and a cap pulled down
far on my head, no one could delineate me from Barney Oldfield.

Have you ever had a car repaired? And have you ever balked to the
mechanic before he fixed it, and have you ever come back about closing time when the mechanic was washed up, and did you find it difficult to recognize him? Well, this, I am sure, would work in my favor.

Now let me see what else there is—the accident, and no one can
recognize me, or any of the five men I portrayed in masterminding
the accident, and no one knows I, shall I say, tampered with the truck,
and the truck is running smoothly, or was, I should say, and the tow
truck is out on a routine run. I am completely non-involved. Anything
I did not think of? The truck getting stuck in traffic? No, I told you,
that's why I selected this particular bank, no traffic. What shall I do to
the truck when I get to it? Why I intend, not seriously of course, to try
and fix it. The driver and the guards will be inside protectively guarding their money: theirs so to say, and not anyone's but mine shortly.
I'll open the hood and pretend I'm working with the engine, and ask

the driver to step on the starter, . . . and the engine will crank over and over, and it, unfortunately, will not start and then I'll tell them I think it's a broken piston. No, what's the matter with me? With a broken piston, the engine would not crank over. Let's see, what could be wrong, not points, I shall certainly have a spare set in my tool case, not the starter engine, it wouldn't crank over in that case either. Hmm, perhaps a cracked rotor, no I'd have one of those too. A cracked coil, I should have a spare one, no, not really. I could have one, but I don't. That'll be it, a cracked coil. Now, if I can't start their engine, then I had better pull them to the garage quickly, wouldn't you agree? It's not good to leave an armored car on the street, or even highway. And besides, they'll have to exchange the contents of the van to another better running van to finish delivery and they wouldn't do this on the highway. I'll tow them down the highway toward the garage. Will they suspect this new man.

I doubt it; not when I have an Allied truck, and I knew that they had called, and I knew where they were disabled. Even if they do suspect him slightly, what can they do. They can't get out, because I shall drive a bit quickly and they would necessarily be smeared on the highway like so much jam. They won't be able to drive away, for I shall be towing their vehicle, right to my favorite warehouse, where of course the tear gas comes in quite handily. I'm sure you realize this now. I did not consider it prudent for me to cut through the armor with a metal cutting torch. The zealous guards might have a tendency for anger and prevention and might try to shoot me. And besides, it would take too much time and the Allied people would be out looking for them before I finished, and this would cause quite a commotion around here when they couldn't find them. They will be still locked in and protected, and probably would feel quite smug. But what if they wanted to come out. All by themselves of their own coughing volition, if you get the picture? Me? Well I have a protective gas mask right here on the seat just for that purpose. Science is so wonderful, isn't it? I'll take it with me in the tow truck and snap it on just before I get to the warehouse. Oh, they won't see it. I'll have to leave the warehouse door open so I can drive right in. Oddly enough, I wouldn't want the guards to shoot me if I had to get out to open the door. That trailer truck parked right in the doorway, at the angle it is, hides that open door. No, the police come over here and sit in their cars and waste time in the shadows only at night, when they can't be seen through the ebon quiet. But in the daytime, only a horse mounted patrolman is on duty here, and he has the entire street to guard, and why guard a deserted pier when all the trucks and confusion at the Fulton Fish Market and the Journal-American is boiling only a few hundred yards from here.

I doubt they can shoot me while we're riding, because of the angle of their truck, remember they'll be pointed up in the air as I tow, and besides, that is why I have that little plate of armor right there. It goes in the tow truck behind my head, . . . the rest of me will be fairly well out of harms way because of tools and mechanism on the back of the truck. Anything else? One minute to go, they should be coming around that corner in one minute. That means I have you in half a minute. The seconds tick by very slowly, do they not, one, one, . . . Oh, the gas will be released when I drive over the cans of gas that I've placed on the ground in the far end of the warehouse. It's five hundred feet long remember, so there's not much chance of the gas escaping into the outside air. I'll just wait until the gas overcomes my friends, and they come out of their truck so gladly. Then I round them up, and let them join their friend from the tow truck, all tied and gagged. Oh they'll be found, so will the truck, even if not by Allied, at least when the trailer leaves again in two days. Perhaps they'll even escape by then. I won't tie them too tightly. The armored car, why it will already be open. They have to open it to get out, do they not. My escape? Well, you see, inside, in the shadowy rear of the warehouse, I've already parked another old car, just like this one. They're all the same, 1938 Oldsmobiles. I tell you, it's rather hard to find them, but I found four of them, separately of course, as I outlined before. After I bring the van in and bind the guards I'll just stack, isn't it nice to have enough money to stack. I'll just stack the money into the car and drive out the door, and I'm away. I won't go far though. There's a black 1957 Ford parked two blocks away, fine running, and inconspicuous. I'll exchange the money once more, change my outfit, leave the Oldsmobile, and poof . . .

Oh I don't know, perhaps I'll go to Cannes, . . . the film festival is next week, you know. And I'll be back in the fall for the theater openings. Other than that, I haven't planned anything.

"I've really got to go now", said the old man as he struggled out the door of the old car, an old black car with the purple showing through where the sun faded the color.

He hobbled out on the road and turned and peered down the road toward where he expected a helping hand for this flat tire which he was too feeble to fix himself. He looked at his watch, and then turned over his shoulders "you're the only one who knows. So don't say anything". What? What if the gas doesn't get into the truck? I'll take measures so their truck will be stopped right over the gas containers, and the gas will certainly go into the driver's compartment through the holes that the brake, clutch and accelerator shafts pass through. And from there it will go in through the doorway between the driver's compartment and the portage compartment. What if it doesn't get through? We are not dealing with a rocket, you know. Be reasonable. Those men have to get their air from somewhere, usually through grating on the roof, and where the air goes in, thence also will go the gas.

"Oh here it is, . . . shh", the old man whispered turning his head quickly and watching the large gray tow truck lumber heavily around the far corner. It was two hundred yards away, and it was rumbling closer and closer, looming larger and larger. Beneath it one could see the wheels of another vehicle pressing closely behind it, following it down the street.

Worry and doubt and concern crept across the face of the old man standing in the middle of the road. Suddenly, the second set of wheels shifted quickly to the left, and a low slung Jaguar roared with the hurt of having its accelerator stepped upon. The Jag leapt past the tow truck and around in front of it, sucking wind, rapidly bearing down on the old man standing in the middle of the roadway. The driver of the Jaguar had not seen the old man until he was bearing down on him very quickly. Terror stricken, he swings his car as close to the other curb as possible as the old man, afraid for his life, backed toward his own car. The old man saw the paralyzed face of the Jaguar driver approaching him wide eyed. The old man backed away, his hand behind him groping for his disabled car behind him, as he kept an anxious eye out not only for the Jaguar but for the tow truck that was now only one hundred yards away. The old man backed another step, almost completely out of the path of the onrushing, screaming, screeching Jaguar which was upon him. He backed, . . . and suddenly he felt the overwhelming surprise of amazement as his body sailed helplessly through the air, suspended from the ground, only to suddenly land bluntly and bouncingly on the hard ground. The Jaguar sped furiously toward the highway, and the tow truck following, now came abreast of the old man, the driver laughing, yes actually laughing, chuckling, as he looked out at the old man on the ground, and then he turned and peered forward, steering the tow truck toward the highway and the armored car.

The old man on the ground laughed too, yes, he laughed and laughed, a hearty, amused, young, self-mocking laugh as he sat on the ground watching the tow truck shrinking into the distant background, as he sat on the black asphalt ground where he had fallen after he had tripped over the spare tire as he backed away from the Jaguar.

BUDDIES

The rain was bouncing down on the sidewalk with a hiss and a spray which rose to cover the entire street with a greyish mist which raised a musty familiar smell that reminded Dino of so many past summers. He stood in the doorway of a candy store, the collar of his olive drab raincoat pulled up around his neck, the hair that he kept full on the back of his head touching the tip of the collar. Dino stood watching the red brick wall and the thousand "window eyes" of the building across the street. But as he peered at the building through the mass of falling droplets, his mind was thinking furiously, the building merely a back-drop for his thoughts. The rain even added to his feeling of apprehension . . . yes, the rain and the musty odor, . . . and he remembered himself being with Jim Plaser, a buddy from school, and Jim's girl Phyllis, on the beach last summer when a sudden rain storm enshrouded the white sand, turning the long stretch of almost white earth to a pockmarked, rain flecked mass of brownish mush that caked warmly on their feet as they ran for shelter near the parking lot, their blankets and clothes swept up in one roll which Dino ran with in his arms.

"I'll get the car", Jim called from the side of his mouth as he sprinted ahead of Phyllis and Dino. "Wait in the bus stop", he said, pointing to a little shack on the side of the road.

Phyllis and Dino ran under the roof of the shed and "whewwed" with relief from the rain and from exhaustion.

"It's really coming down", said Phyllis looking out toward the rows of parked cars with rain bouncing off their hoods.

Dino put the bundle of blanket and clothes on the bench and walked to the front of the shed, standing next to Phyllis. Water ran from his curly hair down to his nose and cheeks. He blew his breath upward and dislodged a drop from the tip of his nose.

"Oh, look", said Phyllis, "some guy forgot to put his top up". A Pontiac convertible was being rained into.

"Now he's got a real convertible", said Dino, "converted into a swimming pool". Dino shook his head; drops of water flew off his hair.

Phyllis laughed at what Dino said and was looking at Dino's profile. Dino was aware of her staring at him but didn't turn to face her.

"Oh, you handsome guinea, you", she said as she put her hand in his hair and touseled it.

Dino turned quickly toward Phyllis, anger in his eyes. "Listen, Phyllis, I told you about calling me that once before".

"I didn't mean it, Dino", she said, "honest".

"Alright, forget it", he said, turning forward to look for Jim's car.

"You're still great looking", she said.

Dino turned his head half way toward Phyllis and smiled. As he caught sight of her, she had a soft smile on her lips, but her eyes were given to abandon, . . . as if she couldn't control her look, and that she was fascinated by his appearance. Dino continued to look at her now, more from curiosity than from attraction.

Phyllis continued to look at him; as she did, her hand groped her way into his, squeezing it with a steady pressure. "You're a nice guy, you know, Dino . . . I think you're great", she said, moving a bit closer, not moving her eyes from his.

"I think you're great, too . . . I think Jim's a great guy, too. You make a great couple", he said as he dislodged her hand, catching sight of Jim's car exiting from the parking lot. "C'mon, here's Jim", he said, not looking at her.

"Get soaked, baby?" Jim asked solicitously.

"Kind of", she said, looking over at Dino who got into the back seat.

"Excuse me, pal", said a man behind Dino, "you can't stand here in the doorway, but . . . people gotta come in".

"Sure, okay", said Dino shaken from his musing about the beach. He flipped his cigarette from his mouth into the street where a stream of water floated it away. "Might as well go", he thought to himself as he pulled the collar of his coat tighter around his neck and headed for the brick building across the street.

"Come on up", said Phyllis's voice into the house phone.

"Okay", said Dino. He hung the phone on its cradle and walked to the elevator and got off at Phyllis's floor.

"Hi, Dino", she said with a tremendous smile as she opened the door.

"Hi. What's up. . .?"

"Nothing . . . yet. Come on in".

"I'll leave my coat here—it's wet", said Dino as he took off his raincoat.

"I'll take it", she said. "I'll hang it in the tub. Make yourself at home, have a drink", she said as she walked toward the bathroom which was in the back in a small hallway between the living room and the bed-room—which Dino could see through the doorway. "She has a nice little body", he thought to himself as he followed her as far as the living room door.

"Nice place you have here", he said, settling down on an antique sofa covered with a red velvet.

"You making drinks?" she called from within the bathroom.

"Sure . . . where's the mixings?"

"In the cabinet against the wall".

"What do you want?" Dino called as he found the bottles.

"Whatever you have".

"Sidecar?"

"Fine", she said as she came into the living room.

"Ice?"

"I'll get it", she said, walking into the kitchen.

Dino looked up as she passed him. She smiled and went into the kitchen, consciously shaking her little rear end which Dino didn't care for because it was flat. He also noticed that she utilized her trip inside with his coat to fix her make-up and comb her hair.

"Here's some ice", she said, handing him a bucket of cubes.

"What did you want to tell me that you asked me over?" said Dino.

"Let's sit down", she said, taking her drink and sitting on the couch. Dino sat on the opposite end of the couch and turned to Phyllis.

"Well, it's about Jim and about us".

"Oh? Tell me about it".

"Well, . . . oh, I don't know. It's just, well, I'm not sure if I love Jim anymore . . . That's it. I don't know what to do. I mean, he's a nice guy and all, but sometimes I feel that I don't want him near me. I don't want him to even touch me, . . . and then, when he wants to stay over at night . . ." She took a cigarette from a box on a side table. Dino took a book of matches from his shirt pocket and lit a match for her cigarette.

"Thanks".

"What about when he wants to stay over?"

Phyllis was sipping her drink, her eyes fixed on Dino.

"Well what can I say to him . . . I can't refuse him, but I don't want him . . . I don't even like the way he does it. I can't stand it, . . . he perspires and he smells". She took another sip from her glass.

Dino was dumbfounded. He sipped his drink.

"What can I do, Dino . . . help me".

"I don't even know what to say to that. Tell him, of course. Tell him how you feel, that's about the only thing I can think of. If he's not your kind of man, tell him. That's only fair. Don't play games".

"That's what it is. He's not my kind of man. He doesn't excite me or anything. It's like dead. You're the kind of guy I like and Jim's not like that. I could be crazy about you".

Dino sat apprehensively serene. He didn't want to get involved in this sort of problem. Phyllis slid over and sat right next to him on the couch.

"Oh, Dino", she said, her arm sliding under his, taking his hand in hers. Her head rested on his shoulder. "Dino, I'm crazy about you, . . . you know that". Her breathing was becoming deeper. She twisted her head to kiss him.

"Listen", he said, holding her away from himself, "you like me, . . .

that's your problem. As far as I'm concerned, you're my buddy's girl, and that's it. It may not mean much to you, but it means something to me . . . it means a lot, . . . and I don't need you or don't want you, especially because you're a fickle little chick, and I don't need that. And I don't need you to go to bed with. I'm not that hungry that I'd put down my friend . . . If you don't love him, tell him. But don't bother me".

Tears welled up in her eyes and she began to cry.

"If Jim means nothing to you, he means something to me". Dino was speaking through anger-clenched teeth. "So forget about us. There's nothing to it". Dino got up and walked to the bathroom to get his coat.

"Don't go, Dino, . . . please stay with me", Phyllis pleaded hanging onto his arm.

"Leave me alone, will ya", he said angrily, shaking loose of her grip. He put on his coat and walked to the front door.

"Please Dino", she called as he slammed the door shut behind him.

Dino took the elevator down and walked, mindless of the rain, to the candy store across the street. "Pack of Viceroy", he said to the proprietor. ". . . rotten little . . ." he thought angrily, "regular little unfaithful whore type".

"Twenty-six cents".

"Here you go", Dino handed the man a dollar bill, "and give me some dimes for the phone".

Dino got into the phone booth and dialed.

"Smith and Warren", said a female voice.

"Mr. Plaser, please".

"Thank you".

"Plaser".

"Hello, Jim, Dino".

"Hi, boy, what's happening".

"Listen, I gotta tell you something and maybe you won't like it. I know I'd want to know if it happened to me. You're my buddy, so I gotta tell you".

"Tell me, what's the matter?"

"Alright. I was just at you girl's . . ."

"Yeah", said Jim slowly . . .

"Well, I don't know how to say this, but your girl gave me a big line of nonsense . . . listen, I'm only telling you this 'cause you're my friend and I don't want you to be hurt . . .".

"Go on, go on . . . what happened?"

"Well, she puts her head on my shoulder, and she wants me to kiss her, and tells me not to leave when I walked out, and I'm calling you to tell you . . .".

"You're kidding me, aren't you. . .?"

"No, Jim, I'm not".

"I can't believe it. . . . You're kidding".

"God damn it, what kind of a joke is that. Believe me, I'm not trying to hurt you. I just don't want you to get stuck . . . well, I just wanted you to know".

"Jesus Christ, you're not kidding, are you?"

"No, I'm not kidding".

"But we're so great together, . . . tells me she doesn't need anyone but me, says she loves me".

"I don't know anything about that", Dino lied.

"Listen, I'll call you tonight", Jim said shakily. "I'm going over to her place right now. Where ya' gonna be tonight?"

"Bob and I are going out. We'll probably be at Pete's Place later on".

"Okay". Jim hung up and Dino heard the click on the other end of the line. He shrugged his shoulders and walked out into the nice clean rain.

"Oh, Jim, Jim, how could you even think that of me", cried Phyllis vehemently.

"Dino called me . . ."

"Dino! That's rotten, low-life bastard . . . He came here today . . . sure, he came with one thing on his mind. And when he couldn't get it, his conceited pride was hurt. Oh, Jim, how could you, . . . how could you believe that rat", she cried, throwing herself in Jim's arms.

"You didn't . . . baby, I mean . . ."

"Nooo", she wailed. "Nobody but you, Jim. You're the only one. I wouldn't even look at that greasy bastard. If I see him again, I'll kill him. I'll kill him", she screamed.

"There, there, take it easy, baby", said Jim, holding her closely in his arms. "You cry if you want to. I'll take care of Dino".

Phyllis cried and cried, and soon she couldn't cry anymore. She just sobbed for a long time as Jim held her, and kissed her head. "I'll get him for this baby, for all of it", he said.

"Please don't do anything, . . . please, let him go. Don't fight. He isn't worth it. And I wouldn't want anything to happen to you . . ."

"But baby . . ."

"Please, Jim, no fight. If he's capable of this, he's capable of anything, and I wouldn't want anything to happen to you".

"Don't worry baby, . . . I'll get him".

"Please, Jim, please", she began to cry again, "please promise you won't fight".

"But . . ."

"Please. I don't want anything to happen", she looked up at Jim and kissed his lips softly.

"All right", he said softly, resignedly. I won't . . . Don't cry anymore". He held her tightly and she rested her head on his shoulder again.

"Hey, Dino, Jim wants ya on'a phone".

"Okay, baby, thanks", said Dino getting off the bar stool. "Order another round will you, Bob?" He walked into the back dining room and picked up the receiver off the shelf in the phone booth. "Hello, Jim . . ."

"Listen, you rotten son of a bitch bastard, . . . I got the whole story from Phyllis and if I ever see you near her or me again, I'll kill you. I'll kill you".

"Hold it. What the hell is this? What'd I do?"

"Did you really expect to get back at her for not going to bed with you by telling me that . . .you miserable low life . . ."

"Now wait a minute . . ."

"No, you wait a minute . . . I've got to get back to her. She feels bad about this whole thing . . . That's another thing I'll get you for . . . making her cry . . . Just keep out of my way, punk".

Dino sat in the phone booth dumfounded, holding the dead receiver in his hand. Finally he got up and walked absently back to the bar.

"What's up, man?" asked Bob. "Somebody slip you a Mickey?"

"Kind of. The guy's chick makes a pass at me and I tell him, because he's my buddy and I don't want him stuck with a chick that's on the make. So she tells him I tried to make her, and now he wants to kill me . . . I thought he should know and he believes her lying mouth and he wants to kill me".

"They shouldn't make handsome guys with feelings. It's a contradiction of parts. Don't you know the guy wouldn't believe you no matter what you told him, no matter if you went to bed with her or not. Phyllis can wrap Jim around her finger, and you expect him to believe you?"

"So what are you supposed to do—let him get married to a tramp?"

"So what did you do? You told him and where'd it get you. He didn't believe you and he never will, . . . and you missed out on a good lay . . . So what did it get you—nothing. You even lost on the deal. You told him because you cherished your friendship, . . . and you even lost that".

"That's right, you know. If I went to bed with her or if I didn't, if I told him or not, it wouldn't have made any difference. I could've gone to bed with her and he still would believe her. Maybe I should've", Dino said, laughing hollowly.

"Yep", said Bob smiling a deep meaningful smile, his eyes twinkling slightly. He nodded his head and laughed softly.

TENNIS, ANYONE?

Earth had been spinning in orbit for eons. Its internal fires were cooling from the original burst of energy infused at the inception of its journey through space. Its course had been regular, peaceful, and uninterrupted. Suddenly, on a fine Spring morning, without rhyme or reason, the earth shuddered, almost shattered, stopped, its houses and people scattered as twigs, buildings collapsing, glass shards flying, rivers overflowing their banks. All the elements of nature were transformed from an ordered system of existence into a polyglot mass of rubble.

And then, as suddenly as it had happened, the cataclysm was over, earth rose again, bearing on it now, not glistening, proud civilizations, but splintered carcasses. The course of its orbit was different now, the world was completely reversed.

And from somewhere light years of light years away, a shattering, ear splitting voice, so loud as to fill the vault of the heavens themselves boomed:

"Double fault. That's set point. Match to Rongdfmo".

And the stray sphere that was called earth continued its course, toward a fence of that ethereal tennis court, surely to bounce again in perhaps two or three million earth years.